In memory of Callum R.

ENCHANTED ISLAND

James Shaw Grant

Published by the Stornoway Gazette Ltd., 10 Francis Street, Stornoway, in
collaboration with the author.

© James Shaw Grant 1989

ISBN 0 9508371 4 8

Printed by Stornoway Gazette, 10 Francis Street, Stornoway.

Foreword

This story was written many years ago when the Western Isles were just beginning to struggle out of the deep distress into which the mistaken policies of successive governments had thrust them.

It lay forgotten in a drawer until the publication of a paper, by Prof. E. J. Clegg of Aberdeen University, analysing the marriage pattern in Lewis over a century of almost continuous emigration, confirmed, in cold statistical detail, the background against which the story is set.

Although all the characters are fictional and have no resemblance to anyone I ever knew, the story is based on an incident which did occur and which I have recorded in *The Gaelic Vikings*. The dedication may give Lewis readers of my own generation a clue to the identity of the original "Willie". The original "Meesh" I didn't know except through correspondence.

Whether successful or not, my aim in writing was to try to catch, in an exaggerated fictional way, the spirit of an island that refused to die, because there were those around who could extract laughter and good fellowship even from their own predicament.

In the happier situation which now prevails I hope the story will be read as a tribute to the men and women who kept a little spark of gaiety alive through a long dark night. I am indebted to the "Stornoway Gazette" and their photographer, John Mackinnon, for the view of Rhenigidale on the cover. Rhenigidale is in Harris, not Lewis, and so is clearly not the Crobuie of my tale, but it has its own symbolism in that Rhenigidale, although it knew not Meesh nor Willie, is a real life village which refused to die — despite the encouragement given it to do so by successive governments over many years.

Chapter 1

At the time I am writing of there hadn't been a marriage in Crobuie for twenty years. Nor a birth. The inhabitants had lost the initiative even to die: they just lingered on in an uneventful and interminable senescence, like fruit that ripened but never fell.

The oldest inhabitant had reached a fabulous age, and seemed set for centuries to come. The youngest was not yet thirty, but the onset of old age came early in Crobuie: those who had not escaped to America or Australia by twenty-five had the mark of doom already on the forehead and in the step. Escape thereafter was impossible.

A "bodach" is an old man. A "cailleach" is an old woman. In Crobuie everyone was a bodach or a cailleach from birth. Childhood and the golden years were just part of the process of decay. Life was a long placid waiting for a release that never came.

It was impossible to tell the ages of the women without access to their birth certificates. All alike wore black. The younger ones might have been handsome and fresh-complexioned, if they felt that way, but they knew that life had already passed them by, so they shrivelled up and looked precisely like the rest. An acute observer, who knew the village well, might have noticed that, when they worked together in the peat banks, the younger women, being somewhat more accessible to new ideas, used barrows, while the older ones still carried huge mountains of peat in creels on their backs. Apart from that there was nothing.

With the men it was easier. Just as you tell the age of a horse by the state of its teeth, so you could tell the age of a man in Crobuie by the state of his walking stick. It was the great watershed in life when the growing lad bought his long shafted crook and went striding across the moor to round up the family sheep. By the time he reached seventy or eighty, the shaft had worn down, and he began to stoop. As a centenarian he shoochled about the village bent double from the waist over a tiny stump, as if supported by a tricycle undercarriage. It was not the men who aged, and wore away, but the walking-sticks. The men were old from the beginning, husks without life or prospect, lacking the initiative even to buy a new stick when the old one gave out.

The blight that fell on Crobuie was not greatly different from the blight that fell on other parts of the Highlands, but it was more severe.

For two hundred years the village had undergone a relentless process of unnatural selection. The young and the virile were weeded out by recurring wars, and waves of mass emigration, sometimes forced, sometimes voluntary, but always selective.

The economic basis of life was destroyed by legalised pillage. The landed gentry took the hill pasture for sport; trawlers from Hull and Fleetwood dredged the fishing grounds clean. The boats of Crobuie rotted on the beach until the sand mercifully covered them. The fishermen rotted ashore. Squatting endlessly over the bright peat fires in their thatched cottages, they talked of storms and rescues and miraculous draughts of fish in a heroic Viking past when they had been human beings.

Crobuie might have died then, decently, but a conscience-stricken State set the embalmers to work, preserving the features, and even some of the movements of life, without the essential spirit.

A pier was built to help the fishermen, but it was sited where no boat could use it. There were no boats left, in any event, and no fish, even if there had been boats. A road was built through the village, but no highway authority was appointed to maintain it. The antique village bus was known as "Wedding Bells", because of the noise from the protesting body as it rattled over boulders, and staggered through deepening pot-holes. When finally the battered chassis decided that it had taken punishment enough, the owner left it where it stuck — in the middle of the road. It was a single track road, and the bus blocked it completely, but there was no longer need for a road: no one in Crobuie had the money to buy a new bus; no one from outside had business with the moribund.

Doles and pensions, given indiscriminately, kept Crobuie hovering between life and death, a petrified village, which retained nothing vital from the past, except an occasional flicker of humour, and a disposition to wrangle over trivial matters, such as rights of access to exhausted peat banks, or the depredations of a neighbour's hens.

The village kept vigil by its own protracted death-bed, waiting with complete acceptance for whatever fate the good Lord had in store.

The good Lord, as it happened, was planning a surprise.

Chapter II

It was a bright day in early summer. Crobuie Bay was as smooth as a swatch of Harris tweed, or a blue plate. In the lee, with his back against a peatstack, Meesh puffed contentedly at his pipe. It was one of those rare moments when life is radiantly good, in a placid, passive way.

The sunshine danced on his greying beard as he puffed, and etched the furrows in his weather-beaten brow. Like many of the villagers, he spent his working life at sea, but had been driven home to the grave-yard peace which brooded over his native hills, when the terms of employment were changed to suit urban rather than crofting conditions. Home was a pleasant change from the f'c'sle, but at times he found it irksome.

Behind the peat-stack he felt safe from the watchful eye of his sister, Annie, but the pipe smoke curling lazily up betrayed him, and the door snapped open.

"Have you finished the hoeing?"

Meesh stirred uneasily, like a sleeper at the onset of a bad dream.

"Time enough," he replied guardedly.

"Have you started yet?" asked Annie, advancing, broom in hand, like Britannia on the back of a penny.

"Time enough," countered Meesh again.

"Are you going to start?" asked Annie, relentlessly.

"Time enough," said Meesh with feeling. He could see an eternity of sunny days stretched out before him, with a few hours' leisurely work at the end — the very end. That was how life would be, if he had the ordering of it.

"I can't understand what you're thinking of — wasting a fine day like this," said Annie more perplexed than angry. Although the menfolk had given up the struggle and relaxed, the women were kept going by a fierce house-pride. Meesh curled up like a cat in the sunshine but Annie was seized with a frenzy of cleaning. It was a point of honour to have a swept hearth, and a teapot ready on the hob — even if visitors never came.

"It's too late to start now," said Meesh, a little shamefacedly.

"In the morning you said it was too early!"

"So it was, then. Anyway the weather's going to change. I don't like the sky."

"I don't suppose you do," snapped Annie.

"It has a greasy look," said Meesh, pointing to a thin film of cloud beginning to dull the sunshine as if someone was slowly pouring whitewash into a basin of blue.

"What on earth were you doing all day?" asked Annie, puzzled to know how anyone could take so long to do so little.

"Ruminating," replied Meesh, and a merry smile threatened to break at the corner of his mouth.

"Whatinating?" asked Annie, blankly.

"Ruminating," repeated Meesh. Then he obligingly spelt it.

"R U M spelt rum when I was at school," said Annie. "Take it from me, your days for ruminating are over. If you're staying at home you'll keep sober, and you'll do some work about the place."

"Aye, aye, bosun," said Meesh, saluting gravely.

"Don't swear at me," said Annie, angrily. "I was a good sister to you all these years, and well you know it."

She turned on her heel, and made towards the house, but at the end of the peat-stack she stopped to discharge a broadside.

"If you had the sense to marry when you were fit to marry, it would be better for both of us today."

"Marry!" said Meesh, dropping his pipe with the shock. "I would sooner put my head in a tiger's mouth. That's one form of lunacy I never had — not even when the moon was full."

"What's wrong with marriage, tell me that?" demanded Annie, although she knew it was folly to get involved in an argument with the old sea lawyer she cherished as only an isleswoman can cherish a brother.

"Nothing. Nothing at all. Marriage is all right," said Meesh. "It's what it does to you. That's the trouble."

"I knew a man once . . ." he added, advancing on her, pipe in hand, to emphasise the points in some salty tale.

"You knew a man," said Annie, cutting him short. "It doesn't matter what it is — you knew a man. You make these stories up on the spur of the moment just to get out of a difficulty. There's not a truthful word in your tongue, or a sensible notion in your head. It's just talk, talk, talk, from the time you get up in the morning — and that's late enough — until you go to bed at night — and that's later still. If you want to know the honest truth, there's not a decent, self-respecting, sensible woman, would have you in a gift."

With bowed head, Meesh let the fusilade pass, waiting until Annie paused for breath.

"You!" she said, drawing herself up with dignity. "You're as much use in the house as a canary."

"Nice cheerful birds they are too," said Meesh quietly, and turned away to hide the smile.

Annie was smiling too. She could never be really angry with Meesh. At least, not for long.

"There's no use talking to you — you have an answer for everything," said Annie, making overtures of peace.

"You should have been a minister. There's no one can preach like you," said Meesh, and the pact was signed.

"Now that the sermon is over, what do you want me to do?" he added. "You didn't come out here for nothing."

"Slip across to the Postmaster's with this jug of milk," said Annie, ingratiatingly. "I'm not dressed to go out."

"What's the idea of sending milk to the Postmaster?" asked Meesh, suspiciously.

"His cow is dry."

"Is ours the only other cow in Crobuie?"

Annie was horrified: meanness was one vice unknown in the village.

"You're not grudging a neighbour a wee drop of milk?" she asked incredulously.

"I'm not grudging anyone anything," said Meesh, "but I don't want to insult a man with that." He sniffed with distaste at the jug in Annie's hand.

Although he said no more to Annie, he added reflectively to himself that the Postmaster was hardly a man, by Crobuie standards: he couldn't tar a boat, let alone sail one, and, although boats were no longer tarred or sailed, the ability to handle them was still the measure of all things masculine.

"Hurry," said Annie, handing him the jug.

"I'll go," said Meesh, "but I won't hurry — that's against nature."

He hadn't taken two steps when he turned back again. "If Willie comes, tell him to wait for me."

Annie shook her head. She couldn't understand Willie at all. A brilliant University student, he spent his holidays with an old uncle in Crobuie, instead of with his parents in Edinburgh, and his favourite crony was Meesh.

"I can't think why he wants to waste his time, holding up a peat-stack with a windbag like you," she said.

"Not holding up a peat-stack," said Meesh, gently. "Ruminating, Annie. Ruminating."

"So that's where you got the jaw-breaker," said Annie, triumphantly. "I hope Willie hasn't learned any words from you."

"He's learned a lot from me, the same Willie, and he'll learn a lot yet," said Meesh putting down the jug of milk, as if preparing for a long session.

"You see, there's one sort of learning you get from books. It puts money in your purse, but it doesn't teach you a thing. There's another sort of learning you get in pubs and places like that: it won't put a patch on the seat of your pants, but, by heaven, it teaches you human nature."

"If I was the Minister of Education . . ." he added, filling his pipe again, milk and Postmaster both forgotten.

"Go, if you're going, for goodness sake," said Annie, exasperated, raising the broom to "shoo" him towards the gate.

Meesh went, but in two seconds he was back again.

"What do you want now?" asked Annie, wearily.

"It's Bellag."

"What about her?"

"She's coming up the road like a greyhound. You never saw anything like the sparn that's on her. She's gasping for breath like a stranded cod."

"What's wrong?" said Annie excitedly, as she whipped off her apron, and smoothed her hair.

"Wrong?" asked Meesh contemptuously. "It looks like a juicy piece of gossip to me."

Chapter III

Meesh whistled jauntily as he sauntered down the road. Bellag, round and plump as a ball of wool, shot past him jet-propelled by the urgency of her news. She scarcely saw him.

Meesh turned to watch her progress. Her feet twinkled in and out below her long black skirt, now and then showing a glimpse of scarlet petticoat, like the waterline of a ship as it slices through the waves.

"Boy, oh, boy, she's got it bad," he said to himself as he resumed his journey in high glee.

Annie had gone into the house. There was less risk of her session with Bellag being interrupted there. Bellag burst into the kitchen.

"Oh, Annie, isn't it dreadful," she exclaimed, as she came through the door, and then sank into a chair to recover her breath.

"I wanted to be first to tell you," she said with a gulp, and relapsed into another palpitating silence.

Annie could see it was something unusual, and waited expectantly.

"It's the things they put in the papers nowadays," gasped Bellag. "If I hadn't seen it myself, I wouldn't have believed it. To think that Crobuie should come to this."

"Come to what?" asked Annie.

"What I'm just telling you," said Bellag, annoyed at the interruption.

"You haven't told me anything yet," said Annie.

"Give me half a chance," snapped Bellag.

"Take your time," said Annie encouragingly.

"I was over at the Post Office," said Bellag. Then she paused. She was going to make the most of her news.

"I hadn't a drop of paraffin for the Tilley."

"Yes," said Annie, punctuating another pause.

"He was as slow to get it for me. He doesn't like to dirty his hands with paraffin when he's working on the stamps. But what could I do, when I hadn't a drop in the house?"

"What indeed?" encouraged Annie.

"He came back with the tin, and I looked to see if it was full, because there's a bash on the side of his measure, and sometimes I won't be getting a gallon, although I'm paying for it."

Inwardly Annie groaned. All this fuss about a half-penny-worth of paraffin. Some people got worked up over very little. "Did you get a gallon?" she asked a little frigidly. Bellag was conscious of the icy edge in her voice.

"It's not the paraffin I'm telling you about at all," she said with a flourish, as if she had just produced an unexpected ace of trumps from nowhere, to win the rubber.

"What then?" asked Annie waspishly. They might have quarrelled, but the story came with a rush.

"When he gave me the tin, he looked round to make sure there was no one else in the shop, and then he said, secret like, 'Have you seen this week's 'St Kilda Sun'?' And I said to him, 'What would I be doing with the 'Sun' at this time of day, with the tea to make, and the hens to feed, and my brother, the Missionary, needing a patch on his trousers, and me without a drop of paraffin in the house?' And he looked round the shop again to make sure no one was coming in, and he said to me, 'There's a notice in the paper — a man from Crobuie advertising for a wife.'"

Annie sat down from sheer astonishment. "I just don't believe it," she said. "I just don't believe it." But it was such a juicy morsel, she almost hoped it was true.

"I saw it with my own two eyes. He took out the paper and showed it to me," said Bellag triumphantly.

"It can't be," said Annie, savouring the news like a connoisseur rolling a fine whisky across the palate. "No," she added after a pause, "It can't be — there's no one in Crobuie would stoop so low."

"Low?" said Bellag contemptuously, "There's some in Crobuie lower than the dirt beneath your feet — and he's one of them."

"Who?" asked Annie.

"The man who put the notice in the paper."

"Who is he?" asked Annie expecting the final revelation and the consummation of the whole story.

"I don't know," said Bellag, surprisingly. "He didn't give his name — the trash!"

"If I ever lay my hand on him," she added, making a quick movement as if wringing the neck of a chicken, a service she was often asked to do by more squeamish neighbours.

"What has it got to do with you?" asked Annie in blank astonishment. She had an innocent mind, devoid of malice.

"Am I not good enough for him?" demanded Bellag belligerently. "Are you not good enough for him? Why does any man in Crobuie need to go past us girls to look for a wife in the newspaper?"

"There's something in that," said Annie hesitantly.

"I'm not going to let it rest there," said Bellag. "Neither will Maggie Moogish when she finds out."

Maggie, it was obvious, was not going to be long in making the discovery. Bellag gathered her shopping together. As soon as she unburdened herself to Annie, she was ready for the next port of call, and the joy of being once more first with the news. In spite of her remark to the Postmaster it was doubtful whether there would be any tea, or mash for the hens, or a patch for her brother the Missionary, until every spinster in the village was aware of the insult flung in their faces by some unknown philanderer.

Towards the end of Bellag's harangue, Willie came in unnoticed. He was accepted as one of themselves by the villagers, and exercised the local privilege of walking in without knocking. If he had waited until Anne admitted him, she would have thought him proud and stand-offish, and would have regarded it not as politeness, but as an affront to her hospitality. He stood quietly just inside the kitchen door, and said nothing until Bellag left. She scarcely acknowledged him as she steamed out, mentally rehearsing the monologue for her next performance.

"What's all the flap about, Annie?" he asked when Bellag was out of earshot.

"I can hardly believe it's true," she said, and paused, as if reluctant to break some unpleasant news. "Bellag says there's a man from Crobuie advertising for a wife."

She was genuinely torn between the desire for a piece of gossip with obvious possibilities, and her dislike of any unbecoming conduct. Advertising for a wife was disgraceful, indecent. She would have been happier if the culprit were from Crogorm, on the other side of the bay. Of course, if he had been from Stornoway it would not have surprised her in the least, for Stornoway was worse than Sodom in the Bible, it even had a picture house, and a Town Hall where they held concerts and dances.

"How do you know he's from Crobuie?" asked Willie, breaking in on her reverie.

"The notice said he was."

"Who is it?" asked Willie, excitedly. He knew all the Crobuie bachelors well, and couldn't imagine any of the tough old shell-backs venturing into matrimony, let alone advertising publicly in the 'Sun'.

"The notice didn't give his name," said Annie.

"That's odd," said Willie sharply. "Why mention the village if it's over a box number? There's something fishy here."

Annie missed the point, but she thought it was fishy indeed for quite other reasons. "I never heard anything more disgusting in my life. To think that it should happen in a Christian land."

Willie, who had a philosophical bent, felt like asking what exactly she meant by a Christian land. He had his own ideas on that point, but instead he said rather gleefully, "Bellag was fair worked up. It'll make a sensation when the news gets round."

"It certainly will," said Annie, and then she added unexpectedly, "You're the only man in Crobuie who won't be blamed for it."

"How's that?" asked Willie.

"For one thing you don't belong to Crobuie, and for another you have a girl of your own."

Willie blushed like the heart of a peat fire under the bellows. "Me, a girl? Nonsense!" But all the same he was pleased that his affair with the District Nurse was taken notice of.

"She's a nice girl," said Annie. "You could go a lot further and get a lot worse."

Again Willie was secretly pleased to hear Annie, whom he respected, speak so well of his girl friend.

"Time enough for me to think of that in twenty years. I'm not through my degree yet," he said.

"The sooner you think of it the better," said Annie with unexpected fervour. "Not marrying is the curse of Crobuie. We've forgotten what a wedding is. There hasn't been one here for twenty years. The men in this village haven't the spunk of a flea. That's the truth, and now they start putting notices in the paper."

"It's an odd affair," said Willie, still puzzled by the fact that the advertisement identified the village but not the man. "What does Meesh think of it?"

"We'll hear that when he comes from the Post Office. And here he is," said Annie, looking out of the window. "Grinning like a stocking with the heel out."

Chapter IV

When Meesh came in, he was trying to look as glum as if there had been a death in the family, but there was a merry glint in his eye that gave the game away.

"Oh Willie, Willie, Willie, what a time we're going to have. Life won't be worth living," he began, as bronach* as the man who lost his purse on the market day and hadn't the price of a dram.

"There's half a dozen women down in the Post Office — they were eating the Postmaster alive when I went in," he continued, his face gradually crinkling into smiles, in spite of himself.

"They're fair demented. They were round him like midges, their teeth snapping like a crowd of man-eating sharks. It's pandemonium. There's been nothing like it in Crobuie since the end fell out of the tinker's cart."

"You and your stories," spluttered Annie, as she swept off into the scullery. "You'll be there till midnight chattering like starlings."

"What happened when the end fell out of the tinker's cart?" asked Willie, settling himself in a chair. With Meesh's stories the manner of the telling often had more relish than the matter, and there was nothing to be gained by hurrying him to the point.

"Well you see," said Meesh, "the tinker had a load of herrings, and they fell out — one here, one there, right down the road. Every seagull from Cape Wrath to the Mull of Kintyre was down on them like a flash. You never heard such squawking and squabbling — not even in the days of the Tower of Babel."

"Look at them now," he said, moving over to the window. "Little knots of women here and there, tearing away like gulls at a nice juicy herring."

When Willie looked, he could see an agitated group of black-clothed women round the Post Office door, and another further along the street, with Bellag in the midst gesticulating wildly while the others solemnly shook their heads. He could almost make out what she was saying from the movement of her arms and the horrified faces of her audience.

"We're the herring," said Meesh.

"Us?" asked Willie in surprise.

"Yes. The down-trodden bachelors of Crobuie. All this fuss because some poor devil wants to get married. The village could do with a little new blood. Look at them now," he added, pointing towards the groups of angry women. "And yet they tell you it's a free country."

*sorrowful or dejected.

"Did you ever hear of John Knox?" asked Willie, knowing that theology was not a strong point with Meesh.

"The boxer from New Orleans?" said Meesh confidently. "I was there the night he hammered Jack Dempsey — Madison Square Gardens. What a night! Man Willie, you're a fool, wasting your time in the university when you could be broadening your mind."

"You're thinking of the wrong man," said Willie, chuckling. "I mean the preacher that wrote a book called 'The Monstrous Regiment of Women'."

"That's them," said Meesh enthusiastically. "That's them to the very life. You can't breathe if they say 'no'. You would think it was the end of the world because some lonely old codger put a notice in the paper."

"There's something peculiar about that notice," said Willie, who was genuinely surprised to hear Meesh put in a good word for matrimony. "I wonder who inserted it?"

Meesh opened the scullery door to make sure Annie was not listening behind it. Satisfied, he shut it tightly and whispered confidentially to Willie, "I did!"

"You can't do that sort of thing, Meesh," said Willie, in genuine horror. As a young man ardently in love it struck him as crude. Almost indecent. "It's not fair to Annie," he added.

"It's the scientific method," said Meesh.

"Scientific my foot," said Willie savagely. "That's a lucky dip if ever there was one. An unlucky dip! Marrying someone you don't know anything about."

"Most people do," replied Meesh, sweetly reasonable. "They find out when it's too late. I'm fly for that. I'll find out everything first. I'll see her handwriting. Then I'll see her picture. Then I'll find out if she has anything put by in a stocking. If the prospects are good, then I'll see herself. In between times, I'll find out whether she can wheel a barrow or milk a cow. I'll find out quietly was her father ever in gaol or was her mother bad tempered."

Willie was getting visibly annoyed as Meesh went on, but quite unperturbed, the old salt finished his recital with a little homily.

"Take a tip, Willie — never marry a virago's daughter. She'll either be a chip off the old block, and make your life a misery, or else she'll be like a wet dish cloot, with all the spunk squeezed out of her. Either way, she won't be much use to you."

"She won't be much use to you anyway," said Willie angrily, his romantic soul aflame at the perfidy of his friend.

"You won't get a wife. Take that from me. You have as much chance of swimming the Minch. She'll make inquiries just as surely as you will, and what will they tell her?"

Meesh waited patiently for Willie's description.

"They'll say, 'Him, the good for nothing loafer! The dried up old barnacle! The spinner of doubtful yarns! You would be as good marrying the devil himself, I'm sick and tired of you, Meesh. I'm disgusted," said the disillusioned Willie, slamming his hat on his head, and making for the door.

Meesh was chuckling quietly. "Well, well, well. Some people have very little sense for all their education."

"I have more sense than you have," said Willie like a six-year-old saying 'I'm no great you' to a pal he has quarrelled with.

"There are only thirty crofts in this village, but there are 23 old maids — 24 if you count the district nurse," began Meesh, as if he were explaining something simple to a very dull child.

"Leave the district nurse out of it," snapped Willie angrily.

"Easy, boy, easy," cautioned Meesh, realising that Willie needed careful handling. "If I wanted to get married, would I need to waste money on an advertisement? I could walk in the first door I came to and hang my hat up."

"You flatter yourself," said Willie, still missing the point. He was now at the door.

"Willie, Willie," called Meesh, getting really agitated when he saw that he might lose his friend.

"What do you want now?" asked Willie, still sulky.

"You know the little wooden figures they have. You pull strings behind them and they begin to dance?"

"Puppets," said Willie.

"That's the very word," said Meesh triumphantly. "Man, Willie, you would make a fine puppet. I've been pulling the strings as gently as anything for the past five minutes, and there you are hopping about like a madman."

"It isn't true that you want to get married?" asked Willie, relieved.

"Married?" said Meesh, and his bellow of mirth rang through the house. "I've got the whole village on a string," he said, confidential again, and with an apprehensive eye on the scullery door.

"You've no idea what a dreary ditch this is. There's more life in a dead dog. Rain, wind, clouds, black clothes, sour faces, sermons as long as a skate's tail, week after week, and nothing happening."

"Man, Willie, things are bad, when you're longing for a funeral to break the monotony," he added with feeling.

"So I said to myself, I'll put a charge of dynamite under Crobuie, and there it is."

"Meesh, you're a genius," said Willie, his anger gone, and tears of laughter running down his cheeks. "Who but yourself would have thought of it."

"Twenty-four old maids, and twenty-three bachelors — counting myself," said Meesh. "Just picture it — every woman mad with jealousy and every man scared that he'll be blamed."

"They'll tear each other's eyes out," said Willie gleefully.

"They're at it now," said Meesh pointing through the window at the crowd round the Post Office.

"I'm going to enjoy my holiday," said Willie with conviction.

"That's the idea, Willie. Remember — a straight face when you're talking to anyone, but now and then we'll give the fire a quiet wee poke, just to keep it blazing."

Chapter V

There was little need for Meesh to poke his bonfire. The news crackled through the village like a moor fire in May, when the heather is tinder dry, and the flames roar like a thousand blow lamps when the east wind fans them.

Bellag darted from croft to croft, her plump figure bouncing erratically over the boulders on the rocky road.

"She'll vault the next one," said Meesh ecstatically, as he and Willie watched her push through a gate so violently that she almost took it off the hinges. Bellag drew the line at jumping gates, but, when she cleared a three-foot ditch with a spring, Meesh slapped Willie on the back.

"I would put my shirt on her for the Grand National — with a creel of peats instead of a jockey."

"She's a steeple-chaser all right," agreed Willie.

"But man, you've never seen the Grand National," said Meesh solemnly, "nor the Kentucky Derby. I don't suppose you've even seen a coolie running with a rickshaw in his bare feet in Singapore. That's the worst of a university education, you're steeped in ignorance."

Bellag did not have it all her own way for long. Every time she emerged from a house, she was followed hotly by the owner, off to break the news to someone else herself. The elaborate introduction which tantalised Annie was dropped as Bellag, making the story shorter and shorter, struggled to keep in front of her competitors.

Chrissie Bell MacLuggage, with her foghorn voice, shouted the news across three crofts at a time, more effectively than a public address system.

Maggie Moogish, her jaw thrust out like the prow of a battleship, was almost hysterical with indignation.

"Her nose is sharper than a butcher's cleaver," said Meesh. "Boy, oh boy, what wouldn't I give to hear what she's saying."

When every woman in the village had heard the news, they began to tell it all over again to each other, simultaneously, like a chorus of excited starlings. As the tumult rose, so did the tempers.

Finch, the game-keeper, a surly dog, was on the hill with his telescope. He saw the scurrying to and fro on the straggling village street. He had no idea what it was all about, but he watched the black-clothed figures with amusement. "Like a lot of bloody ants," he said contemptuously, as he snapped the telescope shut and went on his way.

He would not have been quite so amused if he realised how nearly the commotion touched himself. He did not belong to Crobuie, and he made no secret of the fact that he disliked the people and all their ways. There was a natural enmity between him and the menfolk, to whom poaching was not so much a sport, or a business, as a religion.

The women had another reason for disliking him. Finch spent much of his time on the prowl at night, and rumour had it that it was not all spent by the river. If misadventure befell a girl anywhere for twenty miles around Crobuie, Finch was blamed. The stories were exaggerated, but they had a kernel of truth. Disapproval of his conduct on moral grounds by the strait-laced women of Crobuie was re-inforced by the natural, though suppressed and unrecognised, jealousy of those who are passed by.

It was Maggie Moogish who first saw Finch's unmistakeable hand in the advertisement. Her house was on the outskirts of the village not far from the game-keeper's cottage. She was sometimes oppressively conscious of his movements, especially when he went crunching by in the darkness. It was on these occasions that her uncle, Cold Murdo, felt the fury of his niece's tongue.

Cold Murdo had no idea what caused his niece's temper. He tried to relate the periodic outbursts, to the phases of the moon, the state of the tide, the direction of the wind, or his own conduct, but he could find no pattern or explanation. To him the sound of Finch's footsteps on the loose gravel of the roadway raised only one train of thought, "Which way is he going? Is he likely to be long?" If it had always been safe to go poaching when Finch went by, Cold Murdo might have thought his niece disapproved of that, but whether he poached or not, made little difference to Maggie's mood.

"I think she has the second sight," he once confided to Meesh. "If the mere idea of poaching crosses my mind, her claws are out and she spits like a cat."

"Aye," said Meesh. "It's a queer thing heredity, and it was very thoughtless of your sister to die on you when her daughter had so much of it."

"It's that trash of a game-keeper," Maggie declared as soon as she heard Bellag's story.

"He's wicked enough for it," agreed Bellag heartily.

"It's not fair to say it when we don't know for sure," said Annie, the fairminded, as she joined the gathering.

"That's what I say, too," said Katag, the Postmaster's sister, in a burst of generosity which she had reason to regret before many days had gone by.

"Have you ever seen his kitchen?" asked Maggie with apparent irrelevance. "If ever a man needed someone to look after him!"

"It's true," said Bellag. "His clothes are all over the place as if the sea had washed them up."

"When did you see his clothes?" asked Maggie, darkly suspicious.

"Never you mind," said Bellag with a toss of the head. Lightning flashed between them.

"Clothes don't prove anything," said Annie. "My own brother lets everything lie where it falls. I'm going round behind him all day long picking things up."

"So am I, with the Postmaster," said Katag — she always referred to her brother by his official position rather than his name, it was more distinctive in Crobuie than an earldom.

"We haven't a thing on Finch," insisted Annie.

"Have we not?" asked Maggie belligerently, her tiff with Bellag forgotten. "Who else in Crobuie has the spunk to get married? Not one of them! If you even look at them they sneak off sideways like a crab."

"That's true, anyway," said Bellag, anxious to make the peace with Maggie, like everyone else in Crobuie who had ever crossed swords with her.

"It's not the Crobuie way," said Maggie, and the argument appealed to their parochial pride. "Besides they're too mean to spend the money."

By now they were beginning to be persuaded, and as each in turn abused the poor game-keeper for real or imaginary faults they became more and more convinced that he was the author of the latest crime. Even Annie began to feel there might be something in it.

"It won't be very nice for you having a strange woman in the keeper's cottage," she said to Maggie. "You have trouble enough with himself and the dogs."

"There will be no woman in the game-keeper's cottage," said Maggie decisively. "He may be a big man, but he's only one and there's twenty-three of us."

Maggie snapped out orders like Napoleon on the field of Austerlitz.

"She's calling up the artillery," said Meesh. "The heavy stuff." He read her waving arms as easily as if she had been using semaphore.

"What are you driving at?" asked Willie.

"You watch," said Meesh. "If only we had a telescope for hearing with," he added regretfully. "That would be a really useful invention."

The group scattered as if a bomb had burst in their midst: every woman hobbling off towards home as fast as the road and her corns would permit. A few moments later they came out again, with shawls flung over their shoulders, armed with sticks, pokers, hay-forks, graips, whatever weapon was to hand. Maggie had an old flail, with vicious leather thongs. Catriona Winter had a rusty Russian bayonet picked up at Balaclava.

Winter, her brother, was the oldest man in the village, and no one was quite sure whether he had picked the bayonet up himself, or whether his father or grandfather had brought it home. Winter's bayonet was a frequent source of argument at ceilidhs in the long dark nights. Dates were bandied about in a confused chronology of Crobuie's own, odd scraps of ill-digested history were regurgitated on one side or the other, but the argument never reached an end. Winter unfortunately could not settle it himself: the Crimean war was so long ago, he had quite forgotten whether he was there or not.

Annie dashed in and grabbed the broom. Meesh smiled. It was her favourite weapon, although she never really went beyond a humorous gesture.

"You better do something to save the game-keeper," she shouted, inconsistently, as she gathered her armour for the fray.

"Why?" asked Meesh with utter innocence.

"We're going to strip him naked, and roll him in a peat bog," said Annie. Then she added urgently, "For heaven's sake, don't let us do it."

"Peat's a waste of time," said Meesh. "It washes off."

"This is serious," said Annie. "He'll get his death of cold."

"Why are you going then?" asked Willie.

"Curiosity!" said Meesh. "That's what killed the cat when it fell in the porridge pot."

"I daren't not go — I'm scared of Maggie," said Annie candidly.

"What a woman!" said Meesh with feeling, but not with admiration. "There should be a season for shooting them, the same as for stags."

The door closed on Annie with a bang. There was another bang as she slammed the gate. Meesh watched her scurry down the road, and shook his head gravely. Bellag and Maggie were ordering the troops in two rough lines.

"They mean business," said Willie.

"They do that," said Meesh gleefully.

Willie shrugged his shoulders. He felt the joke was going a bit too far.

"Did you ever see such a shocking sight in your life?" he asked. It was a revelation to see so much malice and animosity boil up among the friendly folk in Crobuie. He had never seen women in a fighting mood before.

"Aye man it's bad!" agreed Meesh, "Bad! Bad!" Then he added unexpectedly, by way of explaining what his worry was. "They're all out of step. They have as much discipline as cows in a thunderstorm." He spoke as if his orderly sailor's mind was offended by the sight.

"You must do something," said Willie sharply.

"Do?" asked Meesh absently. "Haven't I done enough for one day?"

"I mean it," said Willie. "There'll be trouble with Finch. As sure as eggs."

"What do you want me to do — risk my neck to save a game-keeper? I would sooner go bail for the devil."

"Look here Meesh — if he loses his temper he may use the gun," said Willie.

Meesh reached for his walking stick. "Come along, Willie. Or we'll miss the fun."

As they opened the door, they saw the marching column divide to pass the derelict bus, then reuniting, breast the brae and disappear.

Chapter VI

"Maybe we'll be needing the bag," said Meesh cryptically, and disappeared into the barn.

When he emerged, he had the sack in which they carried the net when he and Willie went poaching.

"What's that for?" asked Willie, suspiciously.

Meesh looked at the sky, then down at the bay. "We'll have a good run of fish on the flood tide," he said with evident satisfaction.

Willie was angry. "What about the game-keeper?" he demanded.

"Why worry about him?" asked Meesh. "He has his hands full tonight!"

"There may be murder," said Willie, really worried.

"Anything at all to brighten up the village," said Meesh, unconcerned, as he swung the sack over his shoulder. "I'll carry it as far as Cnoc Fada. You can take it the rest of the way."

"I'll do a lot less," said Willie petulantly. All the same he followed Meesh when he struck across the crofts and out into the moor. He was surprised to see Meesh walk boldly in the open, with no thought of cover, although it was still quite light. Normally they went by devious paths, making sure at every stage that Finch was not in the vicinity. With all his faults, Finch was an excellent game-keeper.

"You'll bump into him, if you're not careful," said Willie. "It's just about his time for supper."

As he spoke, Finch came over the brow of the hill, striding briskly towards home and trouble.

"He'll be having a hot supper tonight, I'm thinking," said Meesh. "Maggie Moogish is the girl to put curry in his rice."

"You'll have a hot supper yourself," said Willie, indicating Finch who was changing his course, so that they would meet by the stepping stones. Meesh made no attempt to get away. He didn't even hide the bag.

"What have you got there?" asked Finch gruffly.

"You're a poor hand at casting a fly," replied Meesh shocked by the game-keeper's lack of finesse. "Man, Willie, hasn't he got a clumsy way of asking questions. As much grace as a cow on a tightrope."

"What have you got in the bag?" persisted Finch.

"Can a man not take home a few peats for his own fire?" hedged Meesh.

"Your peats aren't dry yet," said Finch triumphantly. "They haven't even been turned."

"That's the best of being observant," said Meesh, quite unperturbed. "You have an answer for everything."

"You won't learn that in the college," he added to Willie.

"What have you got in the bag?" demanded Finch, aggressively and for the third time.

Meesh looked at him quizzically for a moment or two.

"If things get too hot, you can always tell them you're married."

"What the hell are you getting at?" asked the bewildered game-keeper, but Meesh had the sack slung over his shoulder and was already on his way.

Finch looked after the retreating figure, chewing over Meesh's words to find the subtle insult he suspected hidden somewhere. At last he gave it up and hurried homeward. He could have a hasty bite of supper, he reckoned, and catch the old rascal afterwards — red-handed. It was a pleasant thought.

Finch, however, reckoned without Maggie, who was down by his cottage, deploying her troops.

Unlike Meesh, the active keeper had his fuel dried and stacked at home. Maggie whooped when she saw the tidy peat-stack. Picking a small black caoran, as hard as a cricket ball, and knobbly, she aimed at a fence post twenty yards away. The peat splintered with the violence of the blow. She aimed a caoran at the next fence post and struck it too. Rapid fire, she struck each post in turn across the end of the garden.

The others joined her and in a moment the air was dark with flying peats, while the stack melted visibly. For six weeks the women had been busy in the peat-banks. Their muscles were like whipcord and their aim was deadly.

"That'll do," shouted Maggie, like a good general conserving her ammunition.

"The water butt, Chirsty," she commanded. Chirsty Bell MacLuggage crouched behind the butt, with an apron full of peats, at the ready.

"The back door," said Maggie. Several of the cailleachs took up position covering the rear of the house.

"You take the main body, Bellag," she commanded, indicating that the peat-stack would provide both cover and ammunition. Bellag and the rest obeyed.

Satisfied with her dispositions, Maggie filled her own apron with selected caorans, doubled it back, and pinned it, to free her arms, then routing out Finch's ladder from the barn, she mounted the roof to survey the field of battle from the chimney head. Peering cautiously between the pots, she saw Finch whistling down the path.

It was not often Finch whistled, but he felt the world was good to him for once. Meesh, the old enemy, was down by the river, like a sitting duck, waiting to be shot.

"Best of all," Finch told himself, "he's got a brand new net." It would warm his heart to hear the sheriff order its confiscation.

Finch paused to light his pipe. Maggie steadied herself against the chimney. The match flickered into life. The caoran sped towards its mark.

With the first, she knocked the matches out of his hand. With the second, she broke the pipe in his mouth. With the third, she stifled the blasphemy that poured from his lips.

Finch dashed for the peat-stack to arm himself, but a fusilade of caorans drove him to cover. He dropped on his stomach and crawled through the heather towards the back door, but on that side, too, the fire was deadly.

He could not understand what had happened. In all the years of conflict with the menfolk of Crobuie no one had raised a hand or even threatened him. It was his job to catch them; they did their best to make it difficult, but, if he succeeded, there was no ill-will.

Sheltering in a ditch, with muddy water oozing through his boots, Finch tried to puzzle it out. Every time he raised his head, a dozen caorans rattled round him. Suddenly he became aware of a movement in the heather. He was being encircled. He leapt from the ditch and ran for his life.

Screaming derisively, the women gave chase. There has been no rout like it in Scottish history since the battle of Prestonpans. Finch in his heyday was a harrier of note, but the women were fleeter of foot than he bargained for.

Bellag, who was nearest, scorched across the moor to cut off his retreat. Maggie, in her haste, came rattling down the roof without waiting for the ladder. In ordinary circumstances she would have broken her neck, but the pent up fury of all the years through which Finch had scorned her, gave wings to her feet, and she sailed uninjured to the ground, striped petticoat and black skirt billowing round her like a parachute.

The yell of triumph raised by Chrissie Bell McLuggage, when the keeper broke from cover, reverberated through the hills, raising a flight of wild duck on the Rushy Loch beyond Crodubh, while at Stornoway airport, fifteen miles across the strait, a puzzled meteorologist wrote "Thunder" in his log.

Christina Winter was beyond running, but she hobbled excitedly in the wake, shaking her fist, and mumbling ancient maledictions from a remote, superstitious past. If she had paused to hear herself she would have been horrified by the vast knowledge of the Black Art which bubbled up from the deep recesses of her memory.

Even Annie, gentle and kindly and dignified, was swept up in the mob, and went screaming across the moor.

Down by the river, Meesh was setting his net, placid, and unhurried. Willie fumed and fretted, but with an artist's eye, and an artist's attention to detail, Meesh went systematically about his task.

"We'll leave the net overnight," he said, abruptly. "He's had enough — poor devil. He won't be around when we come back!"

Meesh made no claim to have the second sight, but he was so shrewd in his judgement of what was happening in the village, Willie sometimes suspected that he had. Chrissie Bell's shout, which reached them as they left the estuary, confirmed his suspicion that Meesh had more than ordinary foresight in the timing of his moves.

"What's wrong?" asked Meesh solicitously, when they met the muddy and exhausted keeper.

"The women have gone mad," gasped Finch. "They're trying to kill me."

"They've been mad since ever I knew them," said Meesh, philosophically, but Finch didn't wait to hear him. Running as if all the wolves in Siberia were panting at his heels, he plunged through the river and up the far bank. Meesh shook his head sadly.

Then, as the pack approached, he tied a handkerchief to a piece of stick, and, waving it like a flag of truce, he took his stand by the stepping stones, barring the women's advance.

For a moment Willie thought Meesh would be knocked over and trampled underfoot, but Annie, anxious for her brother's safety, forcibly restrained the others. They halted uncertainly.

"Man," said Meesh affably, "that's a bad blunder."

"What do you mean?" asked Maggie, struggling to free herself from Annie's iron grip.

"You should never let them run — it makes them tough and stringy," said Meesh.

"What are you havering about?" asked Bellag.

"Perhaps I'm making a mistake," said Meesh with unusual modesty. "I thought, with this shortage of meat, you were putting Finch in the pot."

"It's you we'll put in the pot, if you're not careful," threatened Maggie, but several of the other women began to explain excitedly what they had against Finch.

Meesh listened gravely as if it was all entirely new to him. Finally a slow smile of understanding glowed across his face like a lingering northern sunrise.

"I think I understand now," he said, "but it's still a blunder."

"You mean it's not Finch?" asked Annie, whose early doubts were troubling her again.

"It's not Finch," said Meesh. "I'm perfectly sure of that."

"How do you know?" asked Maggie with a sudden surge of hope. After all, perhaps, one day . . .

"Finch is married," said Meesh, looking slyly from under his great bushy eyebrows, to see how Maggie would take the news.

"Where does he hide her?" asked Maggie sarcastically.

"It's bad, bad," said Meesh sadly. "She left him. Ran away with a draper from Cardiff, a funny little man with bow legs and a Welsh accent. What she saw in the draper, Lord alone knows, but it was a sore blow to Finch's pride. That's why he's so surly."

"The oinseach," muttered Annie, using the expressive Gaelic word for a light-headed, flighty woman. She was quite sympathetic with poor Finch.

Maggie was not so easily convinced. There was more at stake for her and she clung grimly to her hope. "Prove it!" she demanded.

Willie smiled. Meesh, he felt certain, had not reckoned on proof being asked for when he began his fairy tale about Finch.

"That's easy," said Meesh taking the hurdle in his stride. "We'll get Willie to examine the marriage certificate — he's going to be a lawyer."

There was a murmur of assent from the woman. They would take Willie's word for it.

"You'll have a job finding the keeper," said Maggie viciously. "The last time we saw him, he was running pretty hard."

"We'll find him at home, making his supper," said Meesh, quietly. "If you folk used your tongues less and your eyes more, you would have noticed the smoke from his chimney, when he started up the fire." He pointed to a wisp of smoke rising over the hill, so tenuous that most of the women could hardly see it, let alone interpret it.

"Spelded herring," said Meesh sagely, sniffing the breeze. But that was only a flourish to impress the audience.

As Meesh and Willie strode out towards the keeper's house, the women broke into little groups to discuss the news about Finch.

"The trash," said Maggie vehemently. "I've been his neighbour all these years. I kept him in milk when his cow was dry. I fed his hens when he was on holiday. I darned his stockings when he was hard pressed and he never once said draper."

"Why doesn't he apply for divorce, and get rid of the baggage?" asked Annie, the practical.

"Divorce!" sniffed Bellag. "There's many a woman round about will be interested to know he was married all the time."

"That's a true word," bellowed Chrissie Bell McLuggage. "They're far worse than the bachelors — I wouldn't let a married man nearer than ten yards!"

The floodgates opened, and all the stories about Finch's amorous adventures, real or imaginary, came thundering out. It was a thoroughly satisfactory evening, and the women enjoyed it much better than the chase.

Chapter VII

"This is a fine mess," said Willie, as soon as he and Meesh were out of earshot of the women.

"There's great confusion, right enough," agreed Meesh, as if he had nothing whatever to do with it.

"You might as well get this straight," said Willie. "I'll tell no one I've seen a marriage certificate that doesn't exist. A ploy's a ploy, but that's going a bit too far."

"I don't suppose they have a class in lying at the collage," said Meesh.

"I should hope not," said Willie.

"It's a very wide subject, and a very deep subject, and a very important subject," said Meesh.

"And a very unpleasant subject," added Willie.

"You should never speak lightly about serious matters," Meesh rebuked him. "If you were a seafaring man, instead of a scholar, you would not be quite so ignorant."

"We were talking about a marriage certificate," said Willie, laughing. "Never mind the smoke screen!"

"There wouldn't be many marriage certificates, if we all told the truth," said Meesh darkly. "If I was to tell you all I know about lies and liars it would fill one of these things, what do you call them? You have book after book after book, with ABC on the cover?"

"An encyclopedia," suggested Willie.

"That's the very thing," said Meesh. "Give me an encyclopedia, the biggest you can get, and I'll fill it from A to Z with liars."

"I dare say you could," said Willie gaily, entering into Meesh's mood.

"I would say that at the moment you're the biggest liar in Crobuie yourself," said Meesh unexpectedly.

"How do I qualify for that distinction?" asked Willie.

"For one thing you're in love," said Meesh, and the deep-set eyes peeped cautiously out of their caverns to watch Willie's mounting blush.

"Leave my personal affairs out of it," said Willie sharply.

"That's just what I can't do," said Meesh. "When you're in love, your personal affairs can change the colours in the rainbow. All the time you're together you're lying to each other, and all the time you're apart you're lying to yourselves. Man, it would be a cold, ugly, disagreeable business making love if you had nothing to say to each other but the truth. There's not enough truth in Crobuie to cover a sixpence, let alone make love with."

"You're a genius, Meesh," laughed Willie, quite forgiving the reference to his own affairs. "A real, natural genius."

"Thank the Lord I never went to school," said Meesh solemnly. "That would have fair ruined me."

"I'll tell you something, Willie," he added in a sudden confidential whisper.

"Yes," said Willie, expecting something still more outrageous.

"I'm in love myself." He looked sharply round to make sure that not even the corncrake in Finch's croft could overhear him.

Willie laughed. "Why then do you need to advertise?" he chaffed.

"It's not a woman," said Meesh urgently. "Women are bad at any age, but, at my time of life, they're fatal."

"I'm in love with Crobuie," he said, and for the first time that evening, Willie felt that Meesh was being serious.

"So are we all," he responded. "If I wasn't, do you think I would come here year after year?"

"I know you like the place, Willie," said Meesh. "But I've got it bad. It hurts like hell to see what they've done to it. When I think of all the men and women who are dying here before they're born. The place is just an empty shell. They left us the barrel, but they took away the bung.

"There are times when I could cry, walking across the sands after a storm, when the ribs of the boats come suddenly thrusting up, like human skeletons left behind by the tide. You say to yourself, 'that was the 'Fruitful Sea' or 'God's Providence' or the 'Promised Land', and the ghosts of the boats you loved come crowding round you, until you almost think that they're still real and it's you that's dead.

"And then you come up through the village, and look in people's faces. God Almighty, Willie, they're worse than the boats! They walk and talk and eat their food, but all the sap and marrow is gone. They're for all the world like a lot of Egyptian mummies."

It was not often Willie heard Meesh in a serious, let alone an emotional mood, and it passed in a moment. It was the old bantering Meesh who added slyly, "Of course, Willie, you've never seen a mummy."

"I know what they are, for all that," said Willie.

"It's not the same, at all, at all," said Meesh. "You've got to go out into the world and see these things for yourself."

"It's indecent," he added savagely, "keeping human bodies, like herring pickled in a barrel."

"It's all been very interesting," said Willie, "but you still haven't convinced me that I should tell lies about Finch's marriage."

"When you know as much as I do, my lad," said Meesh, "You'll understand. Most people tell lies to make themselves big, or the other fellow small. Or get themselves out of a hole or the other fellow into one. But I'm telling lies to bring the dead to life."

"You better think up a good one for the game-keeper, then," said Willie. "He's in a foul mood."

They had reached Finch's gate, and the game-keeper, who had seen them approach, was standing scowling at the door. One eye was blue and swollen, like a huge, ripe, damson, and there was a lump above the other like a pullet's egg.

"What the hell do you want?" he demanded gruffly, thinking they had come to gloat over his discomfiture.

"A dram," said Meesh sweetly. "I think we all deserve one."

"You can think again," said Finch, as he made to close the door.

Meesh slipped his foot in, keeping it ajar.

"I would never insult a man by refusing his invitation," he explained in an aside to Willie.

Finch put his great weight to the door, but Meesh's foot was as firm as Kebbock Head.

"Take your foot out of there," said Finch jabbing viciously at Meesh's toes with his heavy, iron-shod stick.

Meesh took the first few blows like a stoic, without even wincing. Then he suddenly took his foot away, catching Finch off balance. The door with his own weight behind it slammed shut on Finch's fingers leaving a raw gash.

"His hospitality is overpowering," said Meesh gravely, as he turned towards the gate.

"What about the certificate?" asked Willie.

"I wouldn't go blabbing about certificates if I were you," said Meesh, as if the whole idea had been Willie's.

"They're sure to ask me," said Willie.

"What although?" asked Meesh. "A good lawyer never gives out his clients' affairs. Just you tell them that. They know we've been to Finch's and that's good enough. Besides you can always add that you know for certain Finch is not the guilty party."

"That's easy enough," said Willie gaily. "I happen to know the devil who is."

"We better hurry," said Meesh. "I have a feeling there's fish in the net."

Willie was in great good humour when they reached the estuary. He was having a wonderful holiday.

At that time he was quite unaware that the vindictive Finch was slinking down to the river behind them.

Chapter VIII

There were some fine sea trout frisking in the net, just as Meesh had said. Willie nudged him. "Boy, oh boy, oh boy," he chuckled, using one of Meesh's favourite exclamations.

"I'll take the cliff," he said, referring to the fact that on one side, the estuary was hemmed in by a sheer wall of rock, on which it was difficult to get a foothold, while the other side was more open and easier to work. Meesh generally took the difficult bank himself, because he knew every crevice even in the dark, but it was always Willie's ambition to play the real poacher's part.

"Sooner you than me die of rheumatism," said Meesh, giving Willlie his head.

"I don't see why anyone should die of rheumatism," said Willie in an urgent conspiratorial whisper. They were now coming to the climax of the night's adventure, and instinctively Willie played up the drama.

"You can always rub yourself down with whisky," said Meesh.

Willie laughed. "I'm not going to fall in the river, if that's what you think."

"There are more ways than one of falling in a river," said Meesh darkly, and, with another gay chuckle from Willie, they parted: Willie climbing carefully down the cliff face, in the failing light, Meesh crossed the stepping stones to the far bank.

Everything went smoothly. Willie as sure of his foothold as a mountain goat, got his end of the net clear, and passed the ropes across to Meesh.

"I'll be with you in a moment," he said in a satisfied shout as he turned to work his way along to the stepping stones, and join Meesh for a haul. It was only when he turned that he noticed Finch, sitting on a rock between him and the stepping stones, with a malevolent grin on his face.

"Go ahead," said Finch sarcastically. "Don't mind me." At the same time he moved towards Willie to close the trap.

"It's been a good night's fishing," said Finch with mock affability.

Willie hesitated for less than a second. Then he plunged into the river and swam for the other bank. A few strokes took him safely across and he stumbled ashore, shaking the water from his clothes like a spaniel. His hair, normally brilliantined heavily and sleeked back, hung around his forehead like a fringe of seaweed.

"I hope you didn't wet your feet," said Meesh affably.

"It's Finch," warned Willie.

"Man," said Meesh. "Isn't he having a tough time of it tonight — poachers on top of everything else."

"I think he recognised me," said Willie.

"Maybe he did, but your mother wouldn't recognise you now," said Meesh surveying the bedraggled figure.

"He's here, you fool," said Willie urgently. "He's crossing the stepping stones."

"If he misses his footing he'll be as wet as yourself," said Meesh unperturbed, and resumed his work with the net.

"If you want to be caught, I don't," said Willie angrily, and fled.

"Don't forget to rub yourself with whisky," shouted Meesh, and Willie, in spite of his anger realised that Meesh had foreseen the keeper's arrival and his own misadventure.

There was a crunch of heavy feet on loose stones, and Finch stood over Meesh watching him busy with the haul. Meesh looked casually up.

"I don't think Willie was expecting you," he said.

"So it was Willie!" said Finch. "Thank you very much."

"That was stupid of me. Man it's bad, bad when you start giving information to the game-keeper," said Meesh. But he went on unconcernedly with his work.

"You'll give him more than that in a moment," said Finch. "I'll just take the net and the fish, if you have no objection." There was an edge to his elaborate politeness. Finch was enjoying his triumph. "You have no objection?" he added, sarcastically.

"Not the slightest," said Meesh, seating himself on a large flat stone, and lighting his pipe.

Finch took four fine sea trout from the net, and laid them on the grass.

"It's the best night I've had this season," said Meesh, as if he were entirely satisfied with the evening's events.

Finch made no reply. Expertly he folded the net, stuffed it into the bottom of Meesh's sack, and put his four sea trout in on top.

"Were you ever in Panmunjon?" asked Meesh, affably.

"No," said Finch, curtly, tying the mouth of the sack with a piece of twine.

"Neither was I," said Meesh. "It's one of the few places I've never been to, but if you just sit down on the rock here we can have a little talk."

"It's quite comfortable," he added, when Finch made no move to accept the invitation.

"You can do your talking to the sheriff," said Finch.

"I haven't the pleasure of his acquaintance," said Meesh, sadly.

"You will," promised Finch.

"It's always a change to see new faces," said Meesh. "But I'm afraid I'll be disappointed this time."

He paused for a moment, and looked sideways up at Finch. Finch glowered and said nothing.

"Man," said Meesh. "You got yourself into an awful tangle with the women."

The thrust got completely under Finch's guard. He was still puzzled to know why the women attacked him. "What do you know about that?" he asked, sourly but with a quite uncharacteristic element of amiability. His victory was complete. Meesh had been caught red-handed. The net and the sea trout were irrefutable evidence, and the word of one credible witness was adequate identification. If Meesh bore no ill-will, there was no reason why Finch should. He could relax and enjoy his triumph, and at the same time pump Meesh for information about the women.

Meesh borrowed a box of matches, and, returning it, handed Finch his tobacco pouch. They sat together like old and trusty cronies, puffing contented clouds of smoke across the gently lapping water.

When all the ceremonial of cutting the black twist of tobacco and rubbing it between the palms had been completed, and the pipes were alight, Meesh told a simple, straightforward story about the advertisement, the women's anger, and their natural but mistaken fury against the one outsider in the village as the obvious culprit.

"It's always the strange hen that gets pecked," said Meesh gravely.

"Don't I know it," said Finch, with feeling.

"Man, I thought there was going to be murder," said Meesh, sympathetically.

"So did I," said Finch, rubbing his bruises.

"I had to take drastic action," said Meesh, and he told the story of the marriage certificate.

"You're a real cough-drop," said Finch. "Me married? That's a bloody good one."

Finch laughed at the women's discomfiture. Meesh laughed at the whole mad world which he manipulated so delicately. And the cliffs across the bay joined in for the sheer delight of hearing hearty masculine jollity in a spot where men normally worked in silence, with an anxious eye for the slightest movement round about.

"That'll fix Maggie — for all time," said Finch, and, speaking to Meesh as he might to a father confessor, he told the whole grim story of her long continued assault on his independence. "Poor Maggie!" Finch went off in another burst of laughter. Meesh and the echo joined him and the whole evening rang with voices, until the rock pigeons came fluttering in terror from the Pulpit Cave like the souls of the damned fleeing from the final trump.

"It's time to be going," said Meesh at last, wiping a tear from the corner of his eye. He rose stiffly and gripped the sack as if to take it with him.

"I'm sorry," said Finch, almost apologetically, as he laid a restraining hand on Meesh's arm. "A job's a job!"

Meesh looked at him quizzically. "Finch," he said solemnly, "another word from you and I'll tell them you're a bachelor."

Before Finch could recover, he had lifted the sack and was gone.

Chapter IX

"Did he recognise me?" asked Willie, when Meesh looked in to leave a fish, and find out whether he was any the worse of his wetting. As a law student, Willie wanted to avoid the publicity of a poaching prosecution.

"No," said Meesh. "He didn't spot you at all."

"Good," said Willie. "That's a load off my mind."

"But man," said Meesh, sadly. "Didn't I let your name slip when I was talking to him. It's bad, bad, when a man begins to lose a grip of himself."

It was the first time Willie ever felt Meesh had let him down and he could not keep the flatness of disappointment out of his voice.

"Why the devil didn't you run when I warned you?" he asked.

"And leave the good fish behind?" asked Meesh indignantly.

"You left more than the fish," said Willie accusingly. "You left my name."

"Come here," said Meesh, and he led Willie to the porch to inspect the sack, and the net, and the four fine fish.

"He gave them to me himself," explained Meesh. Willie was incredulous.

"That's right," Meesh assured him. "He's giving us the freedom of the river for all time. We can fish now when we like. But what's the use of that? There's no fun poaching, unless there's someone after you. We'll have to go over the hills now and try the river at Crogorm. People can be very stupid, Willie. A man thinks he's doing you a favour, and all the time he's spoiling everything, like clarting a mess of sticky jam on the good fresh butter on your piece."

"Finch is giving us the freedom of the river?" asked Willie.

"Just that," said Meesh. "We can go as often as we like, and he won't say cheep."

"That's not like Finch," said Willie, still doubtful.

"That's it," said Meesh. "He's not like himself at all, at all. He's got himself into a fearful tangle."

"Telling lies," he added, by way of explanation. "Never tell a falsehood, Willie my boy. It's just like digging the ground from under your feet — the more you dig the more you have to dig. You go on trying to cover one lie with another, until the hole is that deep you would come out in Australia, only hell is in between, and that's a bad place to be."

"That's not what you were saying earlier this evening," said Willie sharply. "You told me I should take classes in lying."

"Never trip a man up with his own words, Willie," said Meesh. "Unless you happen to know what he's talking about."

Willie said nothing. He could see by the way Meesh lit his pipe, and settled down in the old rocking chair by the fire, that there was a story coming.

"The first time I ever went to Tristan da Cunha, there was a great argument in the f'c'sle, when we sighted land. One man said, 'that's it'. Another said, 'that's not it — I know, I've seen it before'. He had seen it before, but it was Tristan da Cunha right enough. It just looked different because we were coming in from the other side. That's the way with me, Willie. I'm always making for the same port, but sometimes I'm on a different tack. You college fellows don't know anything about that at all. You write a few words on a paper and you say 'that's how it is — the professor told me'. That's not how it is at all, it's only how it looked when the professor was looking at it. Everything is different when you see it from the other side. If you went sailing instead of listening to professors you would know that everyone has only two eyes, and you can see only one side of an island at a time but for all that you can sail right round it."

"It's a wonderful subject, navigation," he added reflectively. "The only subject worth knowing. Man it takes navigation to get you into heaven, and what could a professor do for you there?"

The lecture restored Willie's good humour, but he wasn't letting Meesh off with it.

"You haven't told me Finch's lie," he said.

"Man," said Meesh. "You know yourself. Hasn't he put the story all round Crobuie that he's a married man when he's a bachelor all the time. You can't throw dust in people's eyes like that and not get into difficulties."

"Finch didn't tell that story," said Willie. "You did!"

"Just that," said Meesh. "But it was for him I told it."

Willie laughed. Meesh was resentful.

"You know yourself the word for it," he said, "when a man can't go to a meeting, and he sends someone to do the business for him."

"A proxy," suggested Willie.

"That's the very word," said Meesh. "I was Finch's proxy. If it comes to that, I saved his life."

Willie was going to reply but he was interrupted when Habukkuk came hurrying in to break the news.

Everyone in Crobuie called Willie's uncle Habukkuk. Willie himself scarcely knew his real name.

He acquired the nickname because of a violent stammer which shied at "H", "B" and "K" like a nervous horse coming suddenly on a too-high fence.

It was quite a game in the village to engage him in conversation on the lesser prophets of the Old Testament and slyly ask the name of the book which comes between Nahum and Zephaniah. Habakkuk knew it was a game, and played it with zest. While the others led him on to the word he could not say, he exercised a not-inconsiderable ingenuity in dodging it, but always, in the end, he let the neighbours have their laugh.

Habakkuk was one of those happy people who accept themselves as the

Good Lord made them, and join the neighbours in poking not unkindly fun at their own defects. In fact he gave the Good Lord a generous helping hand growing a great drooping moustache, like a silver horse-shoe dangling from his upper lip. It was no adornment, but it added greatly to the laughter in Crobuie to see it flutter when the stammer struck him.

"What's the good of leaving a sea trout here?" he asked morosely as he came in. "There's not a woman in the house to c-c-cook a bit of food."

"They're on the ran-dan right enough tonight," said Meesh with a great bellow of laughter.

"Ran-dan?" said Habakkuk, "the women are on strike. They won't c-c-cook a b-b-bite of f-f-food until they f-f-find out who it is that w-w-wants the w-w-wife."

It was Annie who had the idea first. Maggie Moogish and Bellag had called to discuss the situation after the battle at Finch's.

"Trust that brother of mine to let the fire out," said Annie as the three of them came into the living room. "He hasn't the gumption to put a peat on when he goes out."

"Aren't they all the same?" said Bellag sadly, as Annie flopped on her knees in front of the fire, to gather the embers together and blow them into a blaze.

"You wouldn't think he had hands at all," said Annie. "Except that he can take his porridge and wash is face, and he's not very good at washing."

She resumed the blowing with vigour, venting her spleen on the peats.

"My own uncle is worse," said Maggie viciously. "No wonder they call him Cold Murdo — he never moved fast enough to warm up. And here am I breaking my neck to keep house for him. I was just saying to myself coming up from the well, if the men in this village had to drag home the water the way we have to do, they would have had it coming to the house in pipes long ago."

"Lazy!" she added with vehemence. "When you scold them, they're too lazy even to blush!"

"And it's one of them that has the cheek to advertise for a wife," said Bellag.

That opened the sluice gates.

"Let him wait for a wife then," said Annie. "Let them all wait for wives. Why should we bother slaving for them any longer?"

"That's the very idea," said Maggie, delighted. "The one that likes can take in water, and make the supper, and feed the hens, and wash the dishes, and go to the cruach for peats. Cold Murdo can freeze tonight — I don't care."

"If we all bought pipes and spent the day leaning against a peat-stack smoking the way they do themselves, that would bring the men to their senses, the lazy good-for-nothing lot," said Bellag.

"That's just what they are," said Maggie. "My own uncle is as much use as a crow in a field of corn."

"I'm not too keen on the pipe," said Annie cautiously. "They say it makes you sick."

"It won't make me sick," said Maggie decisively, "but," she added, "you don't need to smoke as long as you don't cook."

Meesh hadn't heard of the strike, or, if he had, he had miscalculated for once. He laughed at Habakkuk's fears.

"Peigi told me herself," Habakkuk assured him solemnly.

"She can't resist a piece of sea trout," said Meesh confidently. "She'll cook it all right."

Peigi did! But neither Habakkuk nor Willie got a bite.

Chapter X

Every man in Crobuie went hungry to bed that night, except Meesh.

An old sailor, he despised housework, and avoided it as much as possible, but he could look after himself when he had to, and he would rather cook than go without. Besides, Annie hadn't the heart to starve him utterly. It was different in some of the other homes.

Bellag hid the pots and pans where the Missionary could never find them. Then, when he was not around, she sneaked out the teapot and frying pan to make a tasty bite of something for herself.

Maggie, being stronger willed, forbade her uncle food, or the chance to cook it, and forced him to the indignity of watching her eat while he went hungry.

Others again let their menfolk loose in the kitchen to see what sort of mess they would make. The hens of Crobuie grew fat and lazy on the failures of the would-be chefs. The men grew lean, and pale, and irritable as the strike dragged on.

The Postmaster was driven to the extremity of making porridge for himself. A man of education, not to say erudition, he read the instructions on the packet with the greatest care, ticking off each step with his fountain pen, as he completed it.

All went well, until he added a generous handful of salt. The porridge was simmering gently on the stove. Little bubbles broke the placid surface here and there, like eyes that winked at him. An appetising smell caressed his nostrils, and signalled messages of hope to his famished stomach. Then when the salt struck it, the porridge rose angrily in the pan, like Vesuvius in eruption, and splattered in his face. Cascades of porridge flowed over the side of the pan, across the stove, and on to the floor. It burnt with an acrid, unhealthy smell, and the cat turned up her nose at the drips.

The Postmaster tried again. Armed with a ready reckoner, a table of weights and measures, an old paper bag and the stub of a pencil, he worked out elaborate calculations of quantities. As a check on his arithmetic he took the Post Office scales into the kitchen, and worked out the problem empirically, with peat dross for meal, and sand for salt. He didn't add water to the mixture, but he measured it out in a flower glass just to be sure.

The experiment completed, he weighed out the proper ingredients with care, and full of confidence, began again. He took the water more slowly to the boil, and stirred more gently as he sprinkled in the salt. For a moment the porridge winked and smiled at him benignly, and he felt the thrill of Tensing upon Everest or Archimedes in his bath. Porridge was achieved. Then suddenly, the pan spat wrathfully, and the mess flowed to the floor.

Katag was fascinated. For hours on end, she sat knitting in the kitchen, and watched him try with pan after pan. Each time, when the salt was added, there was a fresh eruption and an evil smell. At last she could stand it no longer. When the last pan in the house was dirty, and the stove had vanished under a sticky mountain she darted from the house to share her glee with Annie.

"You never saw anything like it in your life," she laughed. "It said 'salt' on the tin right enough, but it wasn't salt that was in it at all. It's there I keep the Suddy soap."

"My goodness," said the downright Annie, "to think that a man can run a Post Office and not know salt from soap."

Katag's hackles rose. She was prepared to laugh at her brother as a cook, but not as a Postmaster.

"There's not a business man can hold a candle to him, in the whole north of Scotland," said Katag icily.

"It's myself that knows it," said Annie hastily. "Isn't he a marvel with the twopenny stamps."

Katag was mollified, and together they went round the village telling the story with unction, and while all the women in Croubie laughed, the Postmaster made his supper disconsolately on a crust of ancient bread. Katag hadn't the heart to hide the loaf, but the butter was nowhere to be found.

Overhearing Katag's tale to Annie, Meesh set off to investigate. Even he was surprised by the state of the Postmaster's stove, but he didn't show it.

"Man," said he cheerfully, "You've made a splendid map. It's for all the world like the delta of the Irrawaddy."

"Here's the Bassein River," he said, pointing to a broad streak of porridge that reached the floor. "And here's the Yamalaw, and the Irrawaddy itself, and the Dala and the China Bakir."

"Look Willie," he added triumphantly, to his aide. "Rangoon would be about here, just where the splashes meet. I suppose you always thought it was on the Irrawaddy itself. They're dangerous things, geography books. Rangoon is away to the east at the junction of the Hlaing, the Pan-Hlaing and the Pegu."

He stood and surveyed the stove with an appraising eye. "Mandalay," he said, at last, "would be just about the spout of the teapot."

The Postmaster paid no attention to the lesson in geography. "Man," he said, sadly, and with a sense of awe, "I never knew porridge was so difficult to make. If you're not careful it might blow up in your face."

"You should have put a weight on the top of the lid," said Meesh solemnly. "That's what they do in Hong Kong."

The room had filled with people. In spite of their hunger, the menfolk of Crobuie were as curious as cows. When they heard the story of the Postmaster's porridge, they hobbled forth to see the wonder for themselves.

There was no sign on their grave faces that any of them knew that Meesh was pulling the Postmaster's leg. They all liked their bit of fun, but the ritual was elaborate and carefully observed. With a victim like Habakkuk, who entered into the ploy, the laughter was open so that he got his share, but with the Postmaster, who had official dignity to maintain, the laughter was silent so as not to hurt his feelings. There was also, no doubt, the consideration that, if they laughed aloud, he might be on his guard the next time, and one of the richest pleasures would be gone from life.

"I always thought the Chinese ate rice!" said Willie gleefully, feeling he had Meesh on the hop for once.

"So they do," said Meesh gravely. "So they do, Willie my boy. I've never seen them eating porridge in the north. Round the Gulf of Chihli, for instance."

He paused, then added slyly, "Of course, I was speaking of Hong Kong."

"And I was speaking of China!" said Willie triumphantly.

"Precisely," said Meesh. "The Cantonese are a different people altogether. Their language is as like Chinese as Gaelic is to English."

"As for that," he added, with a grimace. "I would sooner speak with a mouthful of stones."

There was a murmur of assent from the gathering: they all knew that Gaelic was immeasurably superior to the uncouth and unmelodious language of Shakespeare.

Meesh turned to them, as if he was addressing a public meeting on the Mound in Edinburgh or at Hyde Park Corner. "For real blank stupidity," he said, "give me an educated man, every time."

The murmur was renewed, and there was even some hand-clapping. If they could pull Willie's leg, as well as the Postmaster's, so much the better!

"I suppose in Hong Kong the chop sticks are shaped like spoons," said Willie sarcastically.

"No," said Meesh, without a change of countenance. "Like oars."

"And they make the porridge very thick!" said Willie.

"Exactly," said Meesh, "you can cut it in slabs."

Again there was a murmur of assent, and Willie wisely withdrew from the contest.

"Do you think a half pound weight would be sufficient?" asked the Postmaster, tentatively, holding up a piece of Post Office property of that denomination.

There was a confused babble of talk, as the bodachs discussed the issue. Apart from the fact that they all spoke Gaelic, it might have been a session of the United Nations or a particularly lively afternoon at Whipsnade zoo. Beards wagged, pipes were pointed, clenched fists were emphatically pounded into open palms. Once or twice it got so hot that the fists were thrust under other people's noses. An outsider unacquainted with the conventions of a Crobuie leg-pull might have thought they were quarrelling about something that touched them on the quick like the doctrine of predestination or the virtues of the village ram.

"How much oatmeal did you use?" asked Meesh, solemnly.

The Postmaster explained. In response to further questions, he checked his reply against the packet, and against the scribbled notes on the paper bag. Meesh shook his head. All the bodachs shook their heads. What that was supposed to signify was not too clear, but the Postmaster felt that his word was being doubted, and taking out the scales, he weighed the quantity off to let them see for themselves. The cupful or so of meal was handed from bodach to bodach, examined, tasted, commented upon, rubbed between thumb and forefinger, held to the light, and sniffed, in turn, while the Postmaster looked anxiously on, awaiting the verdict. None was forthcoming.

Questions followed about the temperature of the water, the quantity used, whether it was well water, or off the roof, the size of the pan, the order and manner in which the ingredients were assembled, the age, quality, and manufacture, of the salt, and the type of heat applied.

After much learned talk in which terms were used of which the bodachs using them did not know the pronunciation, let alone the meaning, Meesh hesitantly suggested that a chemical analysis of the water would be required before they could give an authoritative ruling, but he recommended a 56 lb weight, to be on the safe side. The self-appointed jury concurred.

For a few minutes the ploy had taken their minds off their troubles but the gnawing hunger soon reasserted itself.

"It's bad, bad," said Meesh mournfully, although he was eating, if anything, better than usual.

"Bad?" said Cold Murdo, "the back of my stomach is eating the front."

"Does she still make you sit and watch her at it?" asked Meesh sympathetically.

"She does that," said Cold Murdo, the martyr.

"At least," said Meesh, "she doesn't make you ask the blessing on an empty plate."

Several of the bodachs concluded that Meesh was more hardly used even than themselves, but the more observant could not help commenting on the well filled cheeks and the slightly protuberant paunch.

"Hush," said Meesh suddenly. "Walls have ears! Let's go for a walk in the open."

The bodachs filed out, anxious to hear his latest plan.

Chapter XI

The bodachs shoochled through the village in twos and threes, sometimes chuckling over the Postmaster's misadventure, but more often complaining bitterly about the ill-usage they suffered themselves. The women peeped from behind curtains and half-open doors wondering what was in the wind. Finally the procession halted in the lee of a little hummock out of sight of the houses. As a precaution against surprise, Meesh posted a sentry.

When everyone was comfortably seated and the pipes were well alight, Meesh unfolded his plan. "We'll have a barbecue," he said.

One or two of the bodachs knew what he meant, but the others were uncertain whether it was a fish, a bird or a vegetable.

"How do you catch them?" asked the Postmaster.

For a moment, Meesh was tempted. He had a vision of the Postmaster shivering on the rocks in the chill of the evening, with a rod and some exotic bait, waiting for a "barbecue" to bite, while the rest of the bodachs stood by with guns to shoot the monster, and tackle to haul the carcass ashore. They might even be persuaded to build a derrick with a few old masts and spars! Those who knew what a barbecue was could be posted on the cliff top with telescopes, to watch for signs of the monster's approach.

The idea had possibilities, great possibilities. Willie saw the wicked glint in Meesh's eye, but the moment passed. Meesh looked at the hungry faces round about him. The men of Crobuie must be fed, and fed quickly, or he might have a death on his hands. Briefly he explained what a barbecue was.

"You'll make the spit," he said to Scanty, the blacksmith, so called because he had more hair on his chest than anyone else in Crobuie had on his face, and Crobuie was famed for its beards.

"I'll do my best," said Scanty, "if you tell me what you want."

The smith had not lifted a hammer or fired his forge for nearly twenty years, there was no work for him to do in the moribund village, but he still remembered enough of his craft to follow the plan Meesh sketched with a stick on the ground.

There was one difficulty. Whenever he forgot a detail, he had to hurry from the smiddy, half a mile away, in order to consult the plan. It never occurred to Scanty to copy the plan on a piece of paper, and Meesh was too busy with his other arrangements to notice the blacksmith's dilemma.

If the men were dying of hunger, the women almost died of curiosity as they watched the blacksmith shuttling back and fore with a worried but determined look. He had a venerable bicycle, on which the tyres had long since perished, and he stotted from pot-hole to pot-hole with a noise like a thousand riveters, as he pedalled up and down the road. Each time when he came to the derelict bus which blocked his progress, he propped the bicycle hastily against it and went off at a jog trot to waste no time.

It was so long since the blacksmith had used his bicycle, most of the women had forgotten its existence. None of them could remember having seen him run before. For years the village had moved like an earthworm dragging its carcass unwillingly along in slow, spasmodic heaves: each new step requiring a pause and a conscious effort. The women would have thought the blacksmith mad, were it not that the same ant-like activity afflicted every man in the village simultaneously, even Winter himself.

"It's a bad year for the fly," said Maggie Moogish viciously — the men looked just like sheep gone frantic with maggots burrowing in their haunches.

"We have a tin of Cooper's dip," said Bellag helpfully, but the smile that greeted her pleasantry was like a watery January sun, lacking in cordiality. The women of Crobuie were worried. There was something unusual afoot, and they didn't know what it was.

When the spit was ready, the men gathered at the smiddy to admire it. It worked quite well, but there was an odd, unnecessary twist in one of the bars, an intricate flourish, that bore no relationship to the rest of the austere design.

"What's this for?" asked Meesh.

"You ought to know. It was in the plan," said Scanty, angrily. It had cost him hours of effort to get that bit right.

"Nonsense!" said Meesh.

"Damn you!" said Scanty.

"Hush," said the Missionary.

Willie suggested that they go and have a look. It seemed the obvious way of keeping the peace, and the whole male population of Crobuie trooped through the village to examine the plan while the women watched and wondered.

If they had come sooner, they would have found that the Blacksmith incorporated in his spit the footprint of an errant sheep, but as, in the interval, a shower of rain had obliterated everything, the mystery remained, and the argument continues off and on to this very day.

When time hangs heavy in the winter nights, someone refers obliquely to Meesh's skill as a draughtsman, or the Blacksmith's weakness for ornamentation. Threats and challenges ring out, and Crobuie settles contentedly for a snug and satisfying row.

But the making of the spit was the simplest problem. The trouble began when Meesh said, "Now for the sheep!"

"That's illegal," said Callum Coe in a panic. "Killing is against the law."

Callum had reason to know. At one time he had been in business as a butcher, in a very modest way. He got a small supply of meat from Stornoway each week, but in the autumn, when the local mutton was at its best, he usually killed a sheep or two himself.

Once, in the early days of rationing, he sent a cheery telegram to the Ministry of Food, "send no meat today I am killing myself."

That message might well have lost Britain the war.

A policeman was sent to Crobuie to investigate the suicide. He was the first policeman ever seen in the village, where serious crime was unknown (at least to the authorities). The shock of his presence was so severe that more than half the villagers were struck instantly dumb and the remainder forgot their English. It was so much easier to be evasive in the mother tongue. Besides they knew the policeman had no Gaelic at all.

He searched, but could find no body. He visited the homes of the villagers who gave him food and drink, but no information. He took a census house by house, and found that someone was really missing. Callum knew that he was implicated in some unaccountable way in the policeman's visit, so he took to the hills by day, returning to the village at night-fall to get some food from the neighbours.

At that stage an enterprising Stornoway reporter told a London daily of the unavailing search. His story was a masterpiece of the journalist's craft. Every statement taken by itself was unassailable, no one could point the finger and say "that's a lie," yet he succeeded in conveying the impression to readers athirst for sensation that a single suspected suicide in Crobuie was really a mass outbreak of ritual murder of the type that became familiar a little later when the Mau Mau terror was unleashed in Kenya.

"Sullen Islanders Boycott the Search?" screamed the "Daily Disaster." "Are the Hebrideans really civilised?" asked an eminent authority in a feature article, which painted an intimate picture of daily life in the Islands, without revealing that the writer had never been further north than Carlisle. Questions were asked in Parliament by the anxious M.P. for an English industrial constituency who had never heard of the Hebrides until he read the article, and was shocked to discover that part of the United Kingdom in the mid twentieth century was still inhabited by kilted Esquimaux who reared their young on whisky, and devoted their adult lives to crime, superstition and immorality.

In response to the public outcry, stirred up by societies for the prevention of this and that, the government was compelled to divert soldiers, sailors and airmen from urgent war-time tasks to search the peat bogs of Crobuie for a non-existent corpse. Innumerable sorties were flown by the R.A.F. The Royal Engineers laid a light railway across five miles of moorland to get boats to a loch for dragging operations. The "Daily Disaster" at their own expense, employed a well-known water diviner to visit Crobuie and search the peat bogs with his hazel twig. As the twig was sensitive to water, and the country round Crobuie is one vast morass, the diviner had a busy time, but he failed to find his quarry, even when Callum rashly stopped him on the moor to borrow a light for his pipe.

The people of Crobuie watched the search with growing incredulity. They knew the whole wide world was mad (except themselves) but still it was astonishing to see it demonstrated on such a scale.

"You would think they were combing a dog for fleas," said Meesh as he watched a search party of Royal Marines fan out across the moor.

"Like the locusts in the Bible," said the Missionary in a voice of doom. He feared Crobuie would be corrupted by the presence of so many foreigners, so obviously unbaptised, or baptised in the wrong denomination, which was worse.

It was this care for the pure, unsullied souls of Crobuie that led him to go to the authorities by night and tell them (in English) that Callum Coe was still alive. A cordon was thrown round his hiding place, and he was taken by jeep in his night-shirt to campaign headquarters — a building erected for the purpose on the lines of an ops room at fighter command, and which still stands on the moor behind Crobuie, the most imposing edifice in the whole Long Island, and the most absurd.

The Missionary, although convinced that his action was justified, felt some of the guilt of Judas as he solemnly identified his friend. He was afraid he would be ostracised for his perfidy, but his neighbours like himself were content to see the locusts go.

The "Daily Disaster" did not consider it necessary to inform its readers that Callum was still alive. Telling the public the facts was not their business. They did toy with the idea of running the story as a resurrection, but decided they might offend a considerable number of readers in the more backward parts of the country where Christianity still lingers. So instead, they created a diversion by attacking the Ministry of Food for permitting the illicit slaughter of livestock in the Western Isles.

"The crofters wax fat, while London starves," screamed the "Disaster."

"Fair shares, means fair shares for all," was adopted as slogan for the new campaign — a slogan the people of Crobuie would gladly have seen applied.

Stung by this public criticism, the Ministry moved into action. Photostat copies of the telegram were circulated through all the labyrinths of the Ministry's innumerable departments. Minutes were written, duplicated, triplicated, and quintuplicated. Memoranda passed from hand to hand like a snow storm on the steppes. The dossiers on Crobuie grew fat and spawned. Staffs were increased to cope with the corresponsence in the offices at Aberdeen, Glasgow, Edinburgh, London, Harrogate and Cheltenham Spa.

Each department sent its own investigators to the scene, and, as one did not tell the other what action it was taking, snoopers snooped on snoopers, and snoopers snooped on snoopers snooping on snoopers, until Crobuie was writhing with officials like a can jam-packed with worms.

There was panic in the village when Callum was arrested. Most of the women were sure he would be shot. The Missionary mentioned him in prayer as if he were at death's door. In truth, he thought Callum was as good as dead, but as prayer for the dead is popery, he maintained the fiction that Callum was alive. The relatives, having no such subtle points of theology to grapple with, went into mourning straight away, adding black arm bands to their black suits, and black crepe to their black hats. All work in the village was stopped.

The Ministry took a serious view of the case. They wanted it transferred from the Sheriff Court at Stornoway to the High Court in Edinburgh where a more adequate sentence could be imposed, but the Scottish law officers refused to make fools of themselves.

A frailly human Sheriff, who got a bit of steak himself now and again, through devious channels, restored perspective to the case, dismissing the criminal with an admonition. The experience however had burnt itself on Callum's soul. To go to Court, even as a witness, carried stigma in Crobuie. To sit in the dock, even if innocent, marked a man for life.

Callum gave up his butcher's business straightaway, and as there was no one in the dying village with the will to take it over, meat disappeared completely from the tables of Crobuie, except for a haunch of venison now and again when stags were in season and Finch could be circumvented.

So it was that Meesh's plans for a barbecue set all the teeth in Crobuie watering, except Callum's, and he was paralysed with fear.

"It's all right," Meesh assured him. "You can shut your eyes till it's killed, and open your mouth when it's cooked."

Callum was not convinced. "If they catch me again, they'll hang me," he said, feeling his throat as if the mark of the rope were already on the flesh.

Again Meesh stifled the temptation to exploit a comic situation: some of the older men were now so faint with hunger they could hardly stand. Life was too urgent even for a bit of fun.

"There's nothing wrong in killing a sheep — they killed them in the Bible," said the Missionary.

"I'm not in the Bible," said Callum. "I'm a poor crofter in Crobuie."

The reply perplexed the Missionary, who had always been of the opinion that Crobuie was the Bible, and its people the chosen race, but, before he could expound his theory, Meesh settled the point.

"Go home," he said to Callum. "We'll send you a few sizzling chops when they're ready, but you're not in this at all."

Callum hurried off as fast as age and famine would permit.

"Why should that be?" asked the Missionary grudgingly.

"Look here," said Meesh anxiously, "there's no time for arguing. If they catch Callum, it's a second offence, he'll get a year in gaol at least."

"And if they catch us?" asked the Missionary.

"We'll get off with six months," said Meesh.

"I have my official position to consider," said the Postmaster.

"So have I," said the Missionary.

"You're excused," said Meesh to the Postmaster, who began to move away briskly, with a smile of satisfaction on his face.

"Of course," said Meesh, "you cannot get any of the chops."

"Why?" asked the famished Postmaster, stopping abruptly.

"You're a justice of the peace," said Meesh. "The chops would choke you."

"I'll stay," said the Postmaster.

"I'm not a Justice of the Peace," said the Missionary cunningly. "Chops wouldn't harm me at all."

"Well stay and eat them," said Meesh sharply. "You're not an official. Besides we need you to say the grace."

The Missionary was unconvinced, but he could hardly refuse a call to duty, publicly, before his whole flock.

It was Habakkuk who raised the most pressing question of all. "Whose sheep will we k-k-k-kill?"

"There's a stray from Crogorm on the pasture just now," suggested Cold Murdo.

"That's stealing," said the Missionary, firmly.

"It's worse then stealing; it's stupidity," said Meesh. "Do you want the Crogorm folk plundering on us, when they're ten to one?"

"What do you suggest then?" asked Cold Murdo with unusual vigour. "We can't all starve while you make up your mind."

Meesh ignored the provocation. "We'll draw lots," he said quietly. "Everyone of you give me something small that you can recognise."

He held out his hand, and the crofters threw in buttons, pins, knives, and other odds and ends. Meesh put them into his scooped bonnet, and shook them up to mix them.

"I'm waiting for yours," he said to the Missionary.

"I cannot gamble," said the Missionary haughtily. "I'll make the draw."

There was a growl of dissent from the other crofters.

"Well, that's a generous offer I must say," remarked Meesh, unperturbed. "It's not often nowadays you see a man making a sacrifice for his principles."

The crofters looked blank.

"The Missionary is offering us a sheep," explained Meesh. "He doesn't approve of gambling."

There was a howl of protest from the Missionary, but those of the crofters still able to move were off at the double. Shrill whistles rang out, and the dogs came bounding from all parts of the village obedient to their masters' call. In a few minutes the whole Crobuie flock was racing in from the moor with a pack of dogs in pursuit. The crofters guided them to the village fank, and plunged into the heaving sea of wool, looking quickly at earmarks for identification, prodding rumps and ribs, to find out whether the sheep were in condition.

Once they had found the fattest of the Missionary's flock, they let the others loose on the pasture again, and prepared the victim for slaughter. Although few of them could boil an egg to save their lives, they found it easy to kill and flay a sheep — that was a man's job. Besides, the sheep was somebody else's.

In a short time everything was ready. In the gloaming, on the machair overlooking Crobuie Bay, squatting on peats as improvised stools, sat all the crofters of the village, except Callum Coe, like a group of bearded pirates from some tale of the Spanish Main. A huge peat fire sent up a ruddy glow, and a column of blue aromatic smoke. But above the smell of the peat smoke, richer and more appetising, was the smell that Crobuie had all but forgotten, the smell of a tender, moor-fed lamb sizzling in its own fat.

Early in the feast Meesh realised that he had made one mistake — he had forgotten to invite Finch, but he brushed the intruding idea aside, and lay back to enjoy himself. There had been no ploy like it in Crobuie for generations. Hunger gave an edge to the appetite; knowledge that they were breaking the law provided a relish of adventure; recollection of the Missionary's discomfiture had the bouquet of a rare, old wine; and the thought of the women eating saps or porridge at home was grace before, after, and during the meal.

"You know," said Meesh at last, "after the blessing, I think we should sing a psalm."

The Missionary was gratified. Meesh was not generally regarded as one of the more religious villagers. Perhaps, after all, the sacrifice of the sheep had not been in vain. The Missionary turned to Meesh. "Which psalm would you suggest?" he asked politely, encouraging the convert.

"The 23rd," said Meesh immediately, and they had almost finished it, singing in Gaelic in the old traditional style, with the Missionary as precentor "throwing out the line," before they realised that it had a special application.

Never had Crobuie heard singing of such gusto as when they came to the words:

"My table Thou hast furnished in presence of my foes,
My head Thou doest with oil anoint, and my cup overflows."

It was only then they understood why Meesh had chosen that particular spot on the machair for their barbecue. They were out of sight of the village, but the cliffs channelled the on-shore breeze, carrying the psalm and the peat smoke and the smell of roasting mutton into every house in Crobuie.

Chapter XII

Long before the psalm was reached, the smell of cooking was working its magic on the women.

Early in the day it had been fun to see the men scurrying to and fro. Then curiosity supervened to spoil the womenfolk's enjoyment. All afternoon they worried and puzzled, argued theorised and discussed. Once or twice they sent out scouts, as they did in the Bible, "to spy out the land," but Meesh's sentries kept them off. Annie was not quite as inquisitive as some of the others, but she went the length of breaking into Meesh's seaman's trunk to get his telescope, and climbing Ben Hough behind the village to bring the conspirators under observation, but, as she used the telescope the wrong way round, it did little to illuminate the situation.

It was the first time anything had ever happened in the village that the women did not know about, stage by stage, as it went on. Normally they knew their neighbours dreams, even in the middle of the night as they slept.

They became so preoccupied with the problem that their nostrils were twitching excitedly long before their minds were ready to receive the message. When the truth reached them, they tried to shut it out. Starved of meat for years, the thought of freshly roasted lamb was a terrible temptation, but their pride and determination were stronger still — at least to begin with.

Bellag was one of the first to weaken: she had more than her share of womanly curiosity. "I'll just go to the door and make sure," she told her visitors. When the door was opened, the smell assailed them more strongly than ever. The will may be strong, but the stomach is stronger, and the nose is a remarkable propagandist.

One by one the women drifted to the door, and sniffed. None of them spoke. None of them admitted defeat, even to themselves, but step by step, as if drawn by invisible strings, they moved towards the beckoning smell.

For the first time in their lives all the women of Crobuie were gathered together in utter silence. Each woman, grimly fighting her personal battle of resolution against appetite, pretended not to see the others, as if that would hide herself, slinking inch by inch through the gathering darkness, towards the machair. Now and then they stopped to sniff the air, like a herd of anxious deer, then moved silently forward, at ever increasing speed. It was the singing of the psalm that broke the spell.

"It's not right standing here and the men taking worship," said Maggie Moogish. No one replied, but like sprinters at the starter's pistol they took the hint and ran. It was all they had been waiting for — the inspired phrase that would enable them surrender without loss of self esteem.

The men had been conscious for some time of the shadows creeping stealthily across the machair. They made no sign, and passed no comment but it gave them an inward satisfaction, adding the richest fragrance of all to a truly miraculous meal.

When Maggie broke the silence and the women came at the run, Meesh led the men in a great cheer. Places were cleared for the women, and in a few seconds they were all squatting by the fire, while the men cut them slices of succulent lamb, dripping with goodness. The women ate without plate, or knife or fork.

It was an historic night. Men sat talking amiably, even with their own sisters. Neighbours, who had been at loggerheads for years over peat banks, rights of access, and straying sheep, sat shoulder to shoulder like life-long friends. Feuds, which had gone on for generations, fathers passing the enmity to sons and grandsons who kept it up even when they had forgotten how it all began, were settled with a handshake.

Annie, long-sighted as Meesh himself, produced a teapot from the folds of her roomy dress. "I was afraid to take milk in case I spilt it," she explained, taking tea and sugar from the pot, secured in a knot of newspaper.

Bellag, without a word, dashed off to get milk — her house was the nearest. It was unheard of for a man in Crobuie to perform such a menial task as taking water from the well, but more than half a dozen competed volubly for the honour of filling Annie's pot.

Chrissie Bell Macluggage remembered the scones she had baked for her own use — fortunately she had a generous hand, and the plateful she produced was almost a meal for the multitude by itself. Maggie had a cake; Bellag, by some sleight of housekeeping, had chocolate biscuits. Every women in Crobuie was able to find something tasty in the larder.

The feeding of the five thousand was a minor miracle compared with the feast which suddenly materialised on the machair at Crobuie on the night of Meesh's barbecue. Nothing like it had happened in the Hebrides since the Park Deer raid, when the rebellious crofters of Balallan marched into the Eiskhen forest, and lived like outlaws on the stags they shot. It reminded old Winter of a camp fire celebration on the heights of Balaclava, during the Crimean War, but though he told the story over and over in his thin, quavering voice, he could not be quite sure whether he had actually been there, had heard it from his father, or had dreamt it all as he dozed before the fire after the heavy meal.

The barbecue will be remembered in local lore as long as Crobuie survives. It will outlive the village in the songs and anecdotes it inspired. There was an ancient bardic tradition in Crobuie. Like everything else in the village, it had been dead for years, but the pleasant evening air, the glowing fire, the succulent smell, and the good companionship, brought the old spirit flickering uncertainly to life.

Cold Murdo was old, wizened and bent; kippered by long exposure to peat smoke. He looked not so much like a crofter as the mummy of a crofter, which had somehow escaped from the sarcophagus and was wandering about the village in a stage between life and death. But, behind the mahogany mask, there was a lively, satiric mind. In his youth, he had been noted for his impromptu off-taking songs about local characters and events.

More than thirty years had passed since the wasp last used his sting, but time stood still in moribund Crobuie, and no one was surprised when he began in a mournful, nasal chant to describe the Missionary, searching the hills for a missing sheep and finding nothing but the smell of roasting mutton hovering round him where ever he went. He followed the smell, like a will o' the wisp, through fathomless bogs of sticky peat that clung to the Missionary's trousers like the best Archangel tar; over mountains that thrust their peaks to the stars, and sneered at the tiny Himalayas. Across the Western Ocean, despite blizzard and tempest; ranging the Texan prairies and the pampas of the Argentine; through measureless space and endless time, the Missionary searched for his missing sheep. There was no barb or malice in Cold Murdo's satire, and the Missionary laughed as heartily as the rest as the song went on.

Then the mood and tempo changed. In the heroic language of the Ossianic lays, Cold Murdo sang of the battle of the two stupid, ugly giants who quarrelled about the design of the altar on which the stolen sheep was sacrificed. There was no mistaking Meesh and the Blacksmith. The phrases rang like hammer on anvil as the singer described the Giant of the Forge; then, with the rhythm of the iorram or rowing song, the giant of the sea was deftly painted: a man of outrageous mischief, as deep as the ocean, as fickle as the winds with salt, caked white, like icicles, on his flowing beard.

Verse after verse flowed on, until every man in the village had been identified by some little quirk or absurdity of behaviour or some amusing incident from the night's events. The men laughed and the women laughed louder, until suddenly Cold Murdo turned his satire upon them.

He described them as a herd of wild deer, made bold by hunger and the winter snows, coming down from the hills to ravage the crofts. Famished and unmannerly, they attacked the food like hoodie crows on a dying sheep, or dogfish snapping the bait from the fisherman's hooks; but the men were like Highland gentlemen, eating with grace and dignity from plates of gold and silver, with napkins of fine linen, and kilted retainers to wait upon them.

The men roared with delight, and slapped each other on the back. The women hugged themselves with secret glee. Cold Murdo's satire hurt them not at all, and, for the first time in twenty years, they felt the warm glow of a living community round their shoulders like a thick, cosy, home-spun blanket.

When Cold Murdo's recital was over, no one thought it odd that Habakkuk produced a melodeon and struck up a lively air. No one saw him go for the melodeon, no one remembered him ever playing it before.

Willie, sitting in the shadows with Marion the District Nurse, was astonished, for he always thought his uncle the most unmusical soul on earth, but, such was the magic of the evening, he passed no comment, but slipped his arm round Marion's shoulder, and they hummed the tune together.

"There's no 'b's or 'k's on your melodeon," said Meesh in reference to Habakkuk's stammer, and Habakkuk himself joined loudly in the laughter. He had the wisdom to regard his stammer, not as a defect, but as part of the whole, round character which made him what he was. He accepted the compliment to his playing, and saw no slight to his person. Nor was any slight intended.

The laughter at Meesh's sally was still echoing round the peat fire when Maggie Moogish began to sing the women's reply to Cold Murdo's satire. No one suspected before that she could sing, or that she shared her uncle's gift of impromptu composition. Warped and twisted by the unnatural blight that had fallen on Crobuie, she was normally a vicious, vindictive, querulous creature, but mellowed by the food and companionship, and the sudden feeling that life was flowing in a normal channel again, her tongue lost its malice, though not its edge.

She described the men as scarecrows in a field, shapeless, spiritless creatures, dressed in rags. One day they decided to get married, but how could a scarecrow win a bride?

She sang of the great debate among the scarecrows on the art of making love. "It's not the clothes that make the man," said one scarecrow looking at his rags. "That's the pity," said another, looking at the rotten stick that held the rags together. At last they decided they were too hopelessly unattractive to get any woman by honest means: they would advertise, and trap the unsuspecting victims into thinking they were marrying men.

Changing the metaphor, she described them individually by headmark, setting off to the market in Stornoway to buy themselves wives as they would buy themselves cows, each armed with a length of rope to lead their purchase home. But when the bidding started, the men were too mean to offer a price, and the women turned up their noses and walked away.

What woman in her senses would marry a man from Crobuie she asked, in a swelling climax? They had nothing to offer but bare homes, and bad tempers. They wouldn't give the women rings on their fingers for ornament, but rings through their noses to lead them to work.

The men cheered when Maggie's song was done, and Meesh's laughter gusting across the ocean, ruffled the hair on the statue of Liberty three thousand miles away. Even Winter laughed, in a squeaky falsetto. He was so deaf, he barely heard a word; so old and wandered, he made nothing of the snatches that did come through, but the mood of the evening had gripped him.

No one could remember afterwards who resurrected the ancient set of bagpipes, or where, or when. No one could say for sure who suggested a reel, or who was the first to hooch, but in a moment everyone was whirling around in the craziest eightsome ever danced.

Old Winter and his sister Christina were too palsied to move of their own volition, but they were caught up in the swirling chain and carried through the steps. The Missionary had never danced a step in his life before — frivolity was taboo — but his sister Bellag, more like a ball than ever as she bounced along, grabbed his arm, and whirled him round until the world swayed drunkenly at his feet, and the stars above were merged in one vast whirligig of light.

Willie and Marion danced as only lovers can, oblivious of everyone except each other. Meesh, buoyant of step as of spirit, cut fantastic capers on the machair when his turn came to enter the ring, and Chrissie Bell Macluggage startled even herself by the gusto of her hooching. Maggie Moogish laughed and sang and clapped her hands as if life for once had no bitter tang.

When the reel was over, they all sank exhausted on the grass. Then the women called for a cup of tea. There was another hasty rummaging of larders. The men blew frantically at the dying peats to rouse them into life again. Laughter cracked round their heads like summer lightning while the feast went on and on.

At last the Missionary rose. "I think we should hold worship again," he said, "seeing we have danced, and sung, and eaten." Everyone was agreeable. The curious, bubbling grace-notes of the Gaelic psalms danced a reel of their own through the still night air as they all sang together, "To render thanks unto the Lord, it is a comely thing."

It was long past midnight, but the Hebridean twilight still lingered. The sun was sneaking round the northern sky just below the horizon, and it was not quite certain whether the pale lemon glow was the end of sunset or the beginning of the dawn. The crowd dispersed in twos and threes. The gaiety was spent, and the quiet reverent mood of the psalms went with them. They scarcely spoke to each other but there was a sense of warmth, and companionship, and life which Crobuie had not felt for many years.

Willie and Marion lingered long at the door of the nurse's cottage before he kissed her bashfully and said good-night.

Chapter XIII

It was a wild night in Crobuie. After the barbecue, everyone went quietly to bed, but in their sleep all the forbidden thoughts, all the surpressed yearnings of a lifetime, came bubbling impishly from their hiding places, and the village lived with a gusto it never knew by day.

Like the Postmaster's porridge, the dreams frothed up and spilt over. Staid elders of the church spent the night (in their dreams) in the most ridiculous and comprising situations, and enjoyed it immensely. Women whose lives had been corseted with the very whalebone of respectability flung discretion to the winds and wantoned through the night with exotic and extravagant philanderers.

There was dancing, revelry, laughter, love-making, kissing and screams of delight. The years rolled off the shoulders of Crobuie, and the village was young again, with all the joy and indiscretion of youth.

Meesh laughed frequently as he slept. He wandered through the village in his dreams, peeping into the dreams of others. The recollections of a lifetime spent in foreign parts, where life has colour and love-making abandonment, gave an exuberance to his dreams of what the others dreamt, that even the originals lacked, outrageous though they were.

Once he wakened in a panic. He dreamt that Maggie Moogish was dreaming of him, and in the dream they kissed. Though he recognised Maggie, she was not like the Maggie of waking reality, but a compound of all the strange and fearsome creatures he had ever seen, with the glistening white teeth of the man-eater, and the innumerable arms of the octopus. Her kiss would snap his head off, her hug would squash him to a jelly. Meesh swam for the surface frantically, through innumerable layers of consciousness, having plumbed ocean caverns of thought deeper than he had ever ventured before.

In the morning he had a head like a creel of potatoes. "Boy, oh, boy," he growled as he struggled out of bed, "it's bad to have a headache when you didn't have a dram."

The whole village suffered an intense hang-over. There comes a stage in a dying community when acceptance of fate softens the harsh process of decay — a sort of anaesthesia of the defeated spirit. Meesh by his prank had stirred Crobuie from its slumber and every nerve was raw. For a few hours the villagers had escaped from their grave clothes, but now the grim reality of life (or rather, death) was with them again, all the grimmer for the contrast.

In the morning the faces were longer, the steps were slower, the black clothes were blacker, than they had ever been before. At day-break the

Missionary burnt his boots. "They led me astray," he said bleakly. "I was dancing."

Bellag said nothing. It is doubtful if she even heard him. She was sunk in despair like every other woman in Crobuie. The Missionary tormented himself with an urgent but insoluble problem: what could he do to expiate his wickedness? At times he thought Meesh must be evil incarnate, but his own sin was greater. Could he be the devil himself?

At last Bellag struggled out of her own melancholy mood sufficiently to realise that her brother was in danger of a breakdown. "What are you talking about," she said to him savagely. "They fine diddled you out of your sheep."

Whether it was intuition on Bellag's part to give him a peg on which to hang his bitter thought — a grievance against others instead of against himself — or whether it was simply that she was so out of sorts that greed for once got the better of her generous nature, there is no means of knowing, but the Missionary's reason was saved as he went through the village complaining to anyone who would listen that he had been cheated by Meesh.

Meesh himself was so depressed, he could find no means of diverting the Missionary's wrath. He meekly handed over a sheep of his own to make the peace, thereby incurring the censure of Annie, who, out of spirits like the rest, wanted to know whether he had nothing to do but feed that whole village from his own small flock. He hadn't even the spirit to reply: he was as flat as last night's beer.

The only active man in the village was the Postmaster. He was up betimes to press his trousers. Official dignity had been compromised the night before and he went through the day's routine as stiffly as if he had a broomstick in his shirt.

"A fine fool you looked," Katag said to him morosely at breakfast.

He might have replied that she looked a fine fool herself, when she missed her footing in the dance and went sprawling across the machair like a spilt pail. But he said nothing: to tell the kettle she was black would hardly whiten the pot. He rose from the table frigidly and went through to the shop to take down the shutters.

Business was slow that morning. No one had any heart for buying: buying smacked of life, and life was indecent. Moreover, they were all too shamefaced about the folly of the previous night to meet their neighbours in the full light of day. For the most part they stayed indoors with the blinds drawn fast.

One of the few to stir abroad was Habakkuk: he slipped out early on some mysterious errand of his own.

His chance came when Peigi, his sister, was busy with the wash. It was the second time that week she had washed the clothes. They were hanging on the line almost dry when she carelessly unhitched the rope and let it all fall in the mud. Every garment was black. Normally the mishap would have broken her heart, but today it eased her. She saw it as a punishment.

She felt that she had tholed her assize with providence, and paid for the previous night's sins. Her spirits rose so markedly that she baked a few scones for tea — plain scones, without currants, and just a hint too much of cream of tartar added deliberately. That was the only concession to luxury made in the village throughout the day, and even it was mitigated by the sharp taste of the scones.

Even the weather wore the cloak of penitence. A brooding grey sky leaned with all its weight on the housetops, and there were great pendulous bags, black with rain, which seemed to trail along the ground before they burst. Some of the older and gloomier inhabitants thought for a time the flood had come again, catching them without an ark.

The low black clouds gave Habakkuk a sense of concealment as he sneaked from the house. He was glad, for he wished no one to see him as he buried the offending melodeon — buried it so deeply that people would forget it had ever been his, had ever existed. And yet he could not bring himself to let go his grip on it entirely. He jibbed at the thought of burning it in the fire, or throwing it into the sea with a stone tied to it, as one might with an unwanted cat. It must be out of sight, but it must still be there. He finally decided that "there" was the bottom of a dry, disused well at the end of his croft, and he wrapped the melodeon carefully in straw and tarpaulin, before lowering it down on a rope. He paused, then let the rope fall with a faint rattle. That was that! But, though the thought was not present to his conscious mind, it was lurking somewhere in the shadows behind that it would always be possible to fish the melodeon up again (if need arose) with a line and hook.

The bagpipes to which the company danced vanished as mysteriously as they had appeared.

Although she did not show it as she went about her duties, the unhappiest person in Crobuie that day was the District Nurse. She thought of herself as District Nurse, and not as Marion, the girl who had been kissed. The kiss meant nothing. Willie had been carried away by the general excitement. He had probably forgotten all about it. It was a dreary prospect: the years stretched out before her with only the memory of a casual, meaningless kiss to cheer her on the road. She saw herself, alone in Crobuie, the last kindly service done for the last patient; when she was too old to start a new life elsewhere, but still too young to die.

Many of the younger folk felt like the nurse: in a living community only the morbid are afraid of death, but in a dying community, the young and healthy are afraid of life.

Willie was bitter with himself, although, unlike the others, he could escape at any time. He had been indiscreet and he did not like it. He felt as guilty as if he had stolen much more than a kiss. That damned old rascal, Meesh, had got him on the hop. Willie wandered aimlessly through the house; he fiddled with his fishing rod until he broke it; he lost his temper with the cat and threw a cup at it, which angered Peigi. Finally he clapped his hat on his head and strode from the house.

He didn't know where he was going, but his steps took him inevitably along the well-beaten path.

"Damn you, Meesh," was his greeting when they met.

The challenge prodded Meesh from his gloom, and for the first time that day he smiled.

"I know what's wrong with you," he said serenely. "I know what's wrong with this whole village."

Willie looked at him, but said nothing.

"Don't look so bronach, Willie, my boy," said Meech. "I know the cure as well."

"Shut up," said Willie. "I'm tired of your nonsense."

"It's the old, old remedy," said Meesh, unabashed. "It never fails — a hair of the dog that bit you!"

"For heaven's sake, let well alone," said Willie. "You've done damage enough."

"That's extravagant," said Meesh. "I haven't had my money's worth."

"Leave them in peace, or you'll drive them mad," said Willie.

"There's more than one way of going mad," said Meesh, and Willie took the point. The whole of Crobuie was far gone in melancholia, including himself. He struggled for a moment against Meesh's lure but then gave in.

"Let's have it, Meesh," he said reluctantly.

"I'm not quite sure myself," replied Meesh. "Chrissie Bell Macluggage has a louder voice but I think Bellag is really more effective. We'll go and see Bellag."

"What are you up to now, you old devil?" asked Willie, affectionately.

Meesh smiled quietly to himself. Then he said, irrelevantly, "There's a little place not far from Pernambuco. We went in there with a cargo of cement. Heaven knows what they wanted with cement, unless they ate it. Anyway there was a high hill at the back of the town, just a solid wall of rock."

"Yes," said Willie expectantly.

"I never heard an echo like it," said Meesh. "Whistle a couple of notes, as if you were calling Prince from the sheep, and it would play you a tune like 'The Deil Among the Tailors' or 'The Mucking o' Geordie's Byre'. Shout half a dozen words in Gaelic and it would preach you a sermon in Portuguese. Man, I often wished I could have tried it with a tune on the bagpipes. It would have been worth hearing what it made of that."

"I still don't get it," said Willie.

"You're slow man, you're slow," said Meesh. "Surely you know by now that Bellag has the best echo in Crobuie."

"I think you mean amplifier," said Willie, laughing.

"No," said Meesh, after a pause for consideration. "The echo I'm telling you about not only had speech but imagination."

"That's the worst of education," he added, as an afterthought, "it teaches you all the big words you can't spell, but it doesn't show you how to put butter on a piece."

"What are you going to say to Bellag?" asked Willie.

"That remains to be seen," said Meesh, setting off down the road with a jaunty step.

"I'm sorry about the sheep: it was just a joke," he said as he took his seat by the fire in Bellag's kitchen.

"It's all right now," said Bellag, whose spirits were beginning to rise a little. Folk's spirits generally did when Meesh was about.

From that they went on to talk about odds and ends of village gossip, seasoned with an occasional joke, or reminiscence of the old days in the village — a favourite topic in a village without a future. Then the Missionary came in, still looking like the petrified figure of hope abandoned, and Meesh used all his wiles to coax a smile from him. Bellag, getting more like her cheery self every minute, backed up his efforts, and, by the time Meesh left, a reluctant thaw was setting in.

When they parted at the door, Bellag gave a sidelong glance at her brother to make sure he was out of earshot. "You didn't mention it to Annie?" she asked Meesh.

Meesh looked surprised, as if there had been nothing in the conversation sufficiently important to tell Annie, or conceal from her.

"I don't know what you mean," he said, with angelic innocence.

"Never mind, then," said Bellag, but, as a precautionary measure she added, "all the same, I wouldn't say too much about it."

Meesh pushed back his bonnet and scratched his head, but he had to turn away quickly to hide the mounting smile. The idea he skilfully planted with Bellag had taken root: it would thrive like the weeds in a rainy July.

By supper time Bellag was ripe. Impatient, preoccupied and touchy, she barked at her brother all through the meal. When the table was cleared, she ordered him to fetch the cow from the far end of the croft. He went out mumbling and grousing. It was no job for a man, but he did not argue with her.

As soon as he had gone, she rummaged in his papers for a writing pad and fountain pen, which she hid in her own room.

When the Missionary came back with the cow, Bellag was relaxed and smiling. She gave the impression that milking a sulky cow was the greatest joy in her life. The Missionary said nothing: women were beyond him, but anyway the change was for the better.

"You were late with a light in your bedroom last night," said Maggie Moogish when she met Bellag in the morning.

"You were late yourself when you noticed," snapped Bellag and went on her way.

It was not like Bellag to be so abrupt, and Maggie returned to her housework brooding deeply.

Chapter XIV

When Bellag came into the Post Office for the fifth time that morning to buy a box of matches, Katag became suspicious. She was keeping shop while her brother, in the privacy of the house, grappled with official papers. There was a thin but steady trickle of customers, and every second one was Bellag.

"Why don't you take a packet?" asked Katag.

"I don't want a packet," said Bellag.

"You bought four boxes already today," said Katag accusingly.

"I know that fine," said Bellag.

"Could you not have carried them all at once?"

"What I can carry is my own business," said Bellag, haughtily.

"You're carrying more than's good for you," was the cryptic reply.

Just then Chrissie Bell Macluggage came in, and without a word, without even waiting for her matches, Bellag stalked out. Katag watched her go.

"It's bad!" said Katag darkly.

"What is?" asked Chrissie Bell, expectantly.

Katag threw the box of matches on the counter. "That is," she said. "The fifth she asked for today, and she didn't even wait to get it."

"The fifth?" asked Chrissie Bell, incredulous.

"The fifth!" said Katag, "in exactly two hours and seven minutes." She looked at the Post Office clock for corroboration.

"You think, maybe?" asked Chrissie Bell.

"What do you think yourself?" replied Katag.

"She has every right," suggested Chrissie Bell, tentatively.

"She has that," agreed Katag.

Though neither of them mentioned it they were both thinking of an ancient scandal about a distant relative of Bellag who was eccentric, even by Crobuie standards.

"I hope she doesn't get worse," said Chrissie Bell.

"If she does, they'll have to put her on a short tether," said Katag vindictively. She was still angry about the matches, especially the last uncompleted sale when she had the trouble but lost the profit.

"I'm sorry for Bellag," said Chrissie Bell, and she meant it, for Bellag was popular in the village.

"I'm sorry for the Missionary," said Katag. "He can't do much for himself poor man, alone in the house." She spoke as if it were already an accomplished fact that Bellag had been forcibly removed.

"Alone in the house," echoed Chrissie Bell in tones of doom.

Repeated in isolation like that, the phrase had a new implication, and they hastily changed the subject, because neither of them wished to let the other know the train of thought it had suggested. The Missionary was by no means the handsomest man in Crobuie, but there were compensations and, if he lost Bellag, he might well be desperate. Chrissie Bell gathered her messages and hurried from the shop.

Meesh smiled as he saw her go. He had been watching all day with his telescope trained on the Post Office door.

Willie found him in his favourite nook by the peat stack.

"Have you nothing better to do than watch a crowd of cailleachs buying tea?" he asked with a faint suggestion of disgust in his voice, when he saw where the telescope pointed.

"Many a time," said Meesh, "I've seen yourself with a camera behind a bit of sacking at the cliffs watching the fulmars spitting at each other."

"That's natural history," said Willie, with a laugh. "Scientific research."

"So is this," said Meesh. "Besides, my birds are more interesting."

"Let's make a report then," said Willie, taking out a scrap of paper and pencil. "What have you seen?"

"I've been watching a little dark bird," said Meesh.

"Any distinguishing marks?" asked Willie.

"A purple feather in the comb. A rosy patch beneath each eye, and a row of browny-yellow spots on the neck."

"The Bellag-bird," said Willie gravely. "She wears amber beads."

"Call her what you like," said Meesh. "She's squat and beamy like a Thames barge, with a high square poop."

"Go easy, Meesh," expostulated Willie. "Is this a bird or a boat?"

"A woman," said Meesh. "She has a good turn of speed, and she's running a shuttle service between the Missionary's house and the Post Office."

"There she goes again," he added, excitedly.

Willie looked, and there was Bellag hurrying down the street to collect her fifth box of matches.

"She won't make port," said Meesh. "You just watch. She'll sheer off when she clears the peat-stack. She'll come back on the starboard tack, or else she'll stop to tie her shoe-lace."

"How the heck did you know?" asked Willie, when Bellag stopped dead at the end of the peat-stack and busied herself with her shoe lace. After fussing about with it for a few minutes, she turned for home with a look of annoyance on her face.

"The revenue cutter," said Meesh. "It's just going in to anchor in the port she was making for." He pointed to Christina Winter hobbling slowly towards the Post Office.

"Katag has it bad," said Meesh. "And now Christina is getting her belly-ful. Chrissie Bell Macluggage got it a while ago."

"Got what?" asked Willie.

"You just look," said Meesh, pointing to Christina as she re-emerged. She was still hobbling, still slow by any ordinary standard, but travelling twice as quickly as when she had gone in. "It fairly puts ginger in the step," he said.

"What does?" asked Willie again.

"A little bit of scandal," said Meesh.

"Scandal, in Crobuie?" asked Willie, astonished.

"About Bellag," Meesh explained.

"What?" asked Willie expectantly.

"I don't know yet," said Meesh, "but I soon will."

"In fact I think I do," he added triumphantly. "Would you like to lose some money?"

"What's the bet?" asked Willie.

"As soon as the shop closes, Katag will be over to tell Annie that Bellag is out of her mind."

Willie laughed. "I'll take you on."

"Right," said Meesh, "a cart of peats to a pair of pyjamas."

"What will I do with a cart of peats?" asked Willie.

"What will I do with a pair of pyjamas?" countered Meesh.

Willie's retort was checked on his lips when he saw Katag close the shop a good ten minutes before the time, and come hurrying up the street.

"What kind of pyjamas do you want?" he asked in a token of surrender.

"I don't want bright stripes anyway," said Meesh. "I won't be wearing them until they straik me."

Before Willie could think of a suitable retort, Meesh was at the gate opening it affably for Katag.

"Woman," said he jokingly. "It's yourself that's the spoil-sport."

"Who has time for sport," said Katag on the verge of tears, "and her best friend going mad."

"Mad," said Katag, raising her hands in a gesture of woe. "Poor Bellag: nothing on her mind all day but buying matches. Seventeen boxes, one after the other, and she doesn't even know she's doing it."

"If she's mad," said Meesh, "it's yourself to blame."

"Me?" said Katag indignantly.

"Yes, you," said Meesh. "All afternoon, she's been bursting to post a letter, and you hadn't the decency to turn your back and give her a chance."

"A letter!" said Katag excitedly. "I better tell Annie."

"Why didn't she post the letter if she wanted to?" asked Willie, as Katag disappeared at the double.

"Just take a look at the pillar box," said Meesh, handing Willie the telescope. "The man that put it there was a genius."

"It's where it always was," said Willie brushing the telescope aside. "I posted a letter there myself this afternoon."

"So did you now," said Meesh. "I should have remembered that."

"And still you didn't notice where it is," he continued, with a faint suggestion of a taunt in his voice.

"On the door," said Willie curtly.

"Exactly," said Meesh. "On the door! If the door is open you can't post a letter without being seen from the Post Office counter. If the door is shut you can't post a letter without being seen from half the windows in the village."

"What's the harm of being seen posting a letter?" asked Willie.

"There's always curiosity," said Meesh. "If a woman writes a letter, the neighbours like to know what's in it."

"You're not suggesting that Katag opens the letters?" asked Willie, aghast. In spite of the Postmaster's little fads, Willie had great respect for his probity and his sister's.

"Not for a moment," said Meesh emphatically.

"What then?" asked Willie.

"Man," said Meesh with a shake of the head, "did they never teach you in the college that facts are fatal to conversation? Of course not. They didn't teach you anything useful. They were busy packing you that stiff with knowledge you soon won't have a hullo for your morning porridge."

A look of irritation flickered across Willie's face, like a summer cloud. Meesh smiled, and went on with his exposition.

"If you know what's in a letter, it's as stale as yesterday's bannocks, but if you know who sent it, but not who to or what about you're on to something good. You know all the lies you can make up yourself, and all the lies the rest of the village can make up, when you tell them, and you add their lies to your lies and your lies to their lies. Man, inside half an hour you could write a book, and maybe there's nothing in the letter but three lines to say the corset doesn't fit."

Willie laughed. "You have a theory for everything, Meesh."

"It's all right for you to laugh," said Meesh gravely. "You're an educated man, but Bellag never had her judgment warped. She knew fine her only chance was to buy something and pop the letter in when Katag turned to get it."

"But why buy matches?" asked Willie.

"You can't buy a boll of meal every time you want to post a letter," said Meesh. "Matches are cheap. Besides they keep the matches on a high shelf: they can't get them without the ladder."

"Surely that gave Bellag her chance," said Willie.

"That's what she thought," said Meesh. "But I was in myself this morning and I told them to keep a few matches handy, beside the black twist. I spent my life on boats, Willie, and it turned my stomach to see yon man on a ladder everytime I wanted a smoke. Katag herself is abler in the rigging."

"You saw Bellag coming," said Willie sarcastically.

"That's just conceivable," said Meesh with obvious satisfaction. "Some folk see round corners further than others, although they only have one pair of eyes."

"One day you'll over-reach yourself, when there's no one about to throw you a lifebelt," said Willie.

"I can swim," said Meesh complacently.

"What do you think the letter is about?" asked Willie.

"Katag would give her two eyes to know," replied Meesh. "So would Annie." He pointed to the two of them coming from the house.

Annie accosted Meesh in the brusque fashion that sister can use to brother without offence. "What makes you think that Bellag was posting a letter?" she demanded. Annie was always careful to establish the facts before building a theory, especially when the 'facts' originated with her brother.

"I don't think," said Meesh, "I know."

"How?" snapped Annie.

"She borrowed a stamp," said Meesh, which as it happened was true.

"That's bad," said Annie.

"I thought it peculiar myself," said Meesh. "After all it's to the Post Office she was going."

Katag was furious. "Does she think I can't keep my mouth shut?" she demanded.

"She didn't say," said Meesh. Then peeping from under his bushy eyebrows with the impish, quizzical look Willie knew so well, he added, "I wonder what she was doing with the new hat?"

"Hat?" gasped Katag.

"Perhaps I shouldn't say 'new'," conceded Meesh. "But I never saw it in my life before. It was a very good hat in its day — all gone to seed with feathers."

"Was she wearing it?" asked the cautious Annie.

"No," said Meesh, with scrupulous regard for the truth, "she was carrying it in her hand."

He felt no compulsion to add that Bellag had no intention of wearing the hat, but was using it to make a nest for a broody hen and a setting of eggs.

"She got it from her sister in Philadelphia!" said Katag, with conviction.

"Many a hat she got before, that she didn't dare put on," said Annie significantly.

"She'll wear this one," said Katag, emphasising the point.

"A hat and a letter!" said Annie driving it home with a sledge-hammer.

"The sneak," said Katag. "Writing to a man she doesn't know — that hasn't even a name, but just a number in the papers like a convict."

"Bellag has an odd notion," said Meesh. "She doesn't think it's a man from Crobuie at all, but a rich man in London wanting a Crobuie wife."

"Whatever gave her that idea?" asked Annie.

"When you come to think of it," said Meesh evasively, "Crobuie is famous for its wives. You'll find them in every corner of the globe, doing well. Yarmouth for bloaters, Russia for vodka, Crobuie for wives."

Meesh spoke with conviction, as if he were quoting a proverb known the world over. Katag smirked at him and coloured slightly: almost the last sign of vitality left in the moribund village was the reflex response to flattery. Annie, knowing her brother better, paid no attention.

"A Crobuie wife will never wear out," said Meesh, "but when I was in Hollywood, man, you changed your wife oftener than you changed your shirt."

"How many did you have?" asked Willie with a sly wink at Annie.

"I'm not the marrying kind," said Meesh. "But I couldn't help seeing what was going on around me. Haven't they got garbage bins on the street lamps where you can drop your wife or your husband like a bit of orange peel."

Wille laughed: that was outrageous even for Meesh. Before he could comment however, Katag broke in bitterly, "To think of that snake coming seventeen times in the one morning with a letter hidden in her bodice."

"If she wants to buy a pig in a poke!" said Annie tolerantly, "That's her business."

"Would you do it?" challenged Katag.

"No, indeed," said Annie. "But if Bellag wants to."

"That's it," said Katag fiercely. "You have pride for yourself but none for the village." She turned on her heel and walked smartly down the path, the gravel rising in little spurts, as she showed her indignation with every step.

When she reached the gate, Katag paused. "There's more than one fountain pen in Crobuie," she shouted defiantly at Annie.

Meesh rubbed his hands with glee. Annie turned sadly towards the house.

They both realised that Meesh had Crobuie on the run. Every woman in the village would answer the advertisement, and fight like a tiger for a man she had never seen.

"For all they know, he might be a hunchback," said Meesh, slapping Willie on the shoulder.

"Yes," said Willie, returning the compliment, "or an old sailor with as much sex appeal as a bit of salt cod."

"It'll be a while before they get round to the letters," said Meesh. "There's a confused sea running at the moment."

He pointed to Katag hurrying to the Post Office to write her letter: Annie, shawl on head, sallying forth to discuss the latest developments with some of her cronies; and, down the street, a regular pilgrimage of villagers making for the Missionary's home burdened with gifts and curiosity.

"I forgot for the moment that Bellag is mad," said Meesh. "They'll think it odd if we don't go and ask for her."

Chapter XV

"Were you ever caught in the Corrievreckan?" Meesh asked Willie as they walked together towards the Missionary's.

"No," said Willie, "But I know all about it."

Meesh shook his head. "I'm not talking about a few words on the page of a book," he said. "I'm talking about a whirlpool where men can drown."

"Yes. It's a tidal race," said Willie.

"It's not the tide that makes the trouble," said Meesh. "It's the two tides meeting."

Willie took the point. "There are half a dozen tides meeting in Crobuie tonight."

"You're sharp, Willie, you're sharp," said Meesh approvingly.

The stream of people going to comfort Bellag (and study her condition for themselves) mingled confusedly with the stream of those who had satisfied their curiosity, and now wished to discuss the phenomenon without the restraint of Bellag's presence.

The two groups signalled each other in passing like ships at sea, and there were many innuendoes in low whispers, much headshaking, and a great abuse of dimly understood medical terms. The fact that no one had been able to see anything at all wrong with Bellag was a great stimulus to the imagination. They all knew she was mad, but only the livelier minds could read the signs.

"It's a bad, bad, case," said Callum Coe, with a sigh. "There's smoke coming from her nostrils, puff, puff, puff, like the blacksmith's bellows." Then, by way of explanation, he added in a whisper, "matches — she's eating them!"

"I had an uncle myself that was bad for boots," said old Winter, who was with him at the time.

"He must have found them tough," said Meesh sympathetically.

"He wasn't eating them," said Winter, without the flicker of a smile. "He was hoarding them. He had them by the dozen, all holes, and the soles falling off. 'I don't want to be barefoot on the day of judgment' he used to tell us."

When Winter had told the story half a dozen times in the course of the evening, he was not quite sure whether it was his uncle or himself who had the mania for collecting boots, but he knew it was a bad case and it happened in Crobuie.

Fortunately Bellag had no idea why she had so many visitors, and, as she liked a stir about the place, she spent the evening cheerfully brewing tea, thick, sweet and tarry, with body as well as bouquet.

"Poor thing," whispered Chrissie Bell, "She doesn't even know she's wrong."

The Missionary had no doubt that the visitors were for himself: paying him respect for the sheep he had so generously sacrificed on the night of the barbecue.

"Their conscience is touched — just the way your own was," he told Meesh, leading him through to the kitchen to view the dozens of eggs, quarts of cream, basins of crowdie, and the huge pats of soft, home-made butter with which the table had been piled by open-handed neighbours.

"All this for one poor ewe?" asked Meesh.

"I had no idea I was so highly thought of," said the Missionary with mingled pride and awe.

Meesh's eyes flashed beneath the eyebrows. Willie read the sign, but the Missionary was lost in admiration of the tribute brought him by grateful and respecting villagers.

"I'll need a creel," said Meesh. "Perhaps Bellag will lend me one."

"A creel?" asked the puzzled Missionary.

"To take this across to Annie," said Meesh, indicating the gifts. "After all I gave you back the ewe."

"The sin of coveteousness," said the Missionary sadly. "Grudging a neighbour his good fortune."

"It's the sin of something," said Meesh, "I'm not sure whether it's theft or soliciting goods on false pretences. It was my ewe they ate."

"It wasn't!" said the Missionary truthfully, "It was mine!"

"Physically," said Meesh, "but not morally."

"You gave me that ewe as a gift," said the Missionary. "Just the way the others gave me the butter and crowdie."

"Have it your own way," said Meesh, indulgently. "You've done pretty well on the deal."

"Not bad," said the Missionary with great complacency. Meesh said no more. He knew the Missionary was an earnest man much given to self-examination and criticism. By nightfall he was brooding like a damned soul over his own iniquity and in the morning, after many sleepless hours he went, contritely, to Meesh and returned the ewe. But before the morning came, many things had happened in the Missionary's home.

In the meantime, the gathering of visitors in the Missionary's house had the ambivalence of a Crobuie wake: everyone was genuinely interested because of Bellag's affliction, but little bits of laughter and fun danced merrily along like flotsam in the dark stream of grief.

The cynic might call it hypocrisy to make bereavement a social occasion but only a lunatic is ever moved by a single simple emotion and there is wisdom in keeping hold on life in the presence of death.

On this occasion the corpse they came to mourn (or rather the invalid they came to comfort) was the merriest of the party. Normally at a wake one is solemn in presence of the corpse and the next of kin; the laughter is surreptitious and comes by way of release when they are out of earshot.

Here the company laughed with Bellag and her brother pretending that all was well and pulled long faces and heaved deep sighs only when they were out of the room.

"It's sad to see her so happy," whispered the Blacksmith mournfully.

"Poor creature," said Chrissie Bell Macluggage. "She'll have time enough for crying when she comes to her senses and finds that she's mad."

"Himself doesn't realise it either," said the Blacksmith indicating the Missionary who had just left the room.

"Maybe he's got it too — it's in the blood," said Chrissie Bell.

"It's in the blood alright," said the Blacksmith.

"Nothing of the sort," said the District Nurse who had just come in. "Bellag is as wise as any woman in the village. Perhaps wiser."

"Can you not see the way she's laughing?" asked Chrissie Bell.

"Why shouldn't she?" asked the Nurse. "A laugh would do us all good."

Marion was a placid girl, not given to arguing. When she heard about Bellag's condition she hurried along to see if she could help, and, finding her in perfect health, decided she was the victim of a cruel joke. She suspected Meesh and was afraid Willie might have a hand in it too. Meesh she could forgive, because that was his nature, but Willie was different: in a way he even involved herself, although their friendship had been cooler since the night of the barbecue. Her sharp rebuke to Chrissie Bell was really aimed at Willie, and Willie knew.

A fierce argument broke out in which the Nurse found herself completely outnumbered. Of the dozen people in the room only Meesh and Willie supported her. They declared that they could see no change in Bellag. Marion was glad of their assistance, but shrewdly suspected that they were merely covering their tracks.

Whenever Bellag went out to get tea for a fresh arrival the battle was resumed. Whenever she returned, the company laughed and joked about other things.

The discussion took a new turn when Maggie Moogish stormed in: Annie had told her of the letter.

"There's nothing wrong with her," she said, emphatically.

"You haven't seen her yet," said Chrissie Bell.

"I will, never fear," said Maggie pugnaciously. "That's what I came for. She's playing daft to hide her wickedness. She replied to that advertisement."

There was a cry of rage and horror from the women. The men laughed so uproariously that Bellag came bouncing in to share the joke. She was hot with fussing over the tea, excited with the flow of visitors: she looked for all the world like a fireball rolling across the floor.

Without warning Maggie attacked. Bellag was deceitful, lacking in womanly pride, untrue to her neighbours, a disgrace to the village. She was more guileful than Eve, more abandoned than Jezebel, more shameless than the women who got their pictures in the papers with cigarettes in their mouths and nothing on their bodies but the skin God gave them.

Maggie surpassed herself. She had an exalted theme — honour — and the most powerful motive of all — jealousy!

"I won't take him now supposing he asks me on his bended knees," said Bellag in tears. All evening, in her expectations, she had been happily married, although the letter was not even posted yet.

"You thought you had him," sneered Maggie. "He wouldn't look at you twice, supposing he found you in his porridge."

Wounded beyond bearing, Bellag struck back. "I wouldn't put it past you to do it yourself."

Like a peal of thunder, rocking the house, the retort brought every woman present to her feet. From Maggie's fury, they knew the shaft struck home — she had written a letter too.

The women vanished. The Blacksmith swore they went through the walls, they were out so quickly. Never since the Chinese invented paper had there been so much scurrying and scrabbling to find something to write with. Rusty, hen-toed nibs scratched across the page. Ancient quills were pressed to duty after many decades of retirement. Cockerels had their tail feathers forcibly extracted when nothing better was available. Chrissie Bell Macluggage split her finger to the bone sharpening a stumpy pencil with a borrowed axe, while old Christina Winter spelled out her letter painfully in letters of soot applied with a pointed stick.

To find writing material was the least of their worries. They were then faced with the task of transmuting the commonplace facts of life into something romantic, to whet the appetite of a cabinet minister, a millionaire, a duke, at the very least, or even, perhaps a film star.

In Crobuie film stars were publicly frowned on as wicked, but to the women in private they were still the most attractive of men (with the possible exception of ministers of religion). As the women had made up their minds that the advertisement originated in London, and there were no ministers worthy the name in that sink of iniquity, they were quite prepared to accept Clark Gable as a consolation prize.

Few of them had photographs they could enclose, so the truth was no clog to their fancy, and they wrote of their charms in the shop-soiled vulgar superlatives of "Heart-throb", "Hollywood's smartest" and the current advertising slogans for bad breath lozenges.

They wrote in a foreign language — a feat which few so-called educated people would attempt — and did it expressively. Unfortunately the picture they painted of themselves was more like the Saturday night crowd in a third-rate Blackpool palais than anything seen in the Hebrides.

That was the real tragedy of Crobuie: the village had surrendered its own best, and accepted the shoddy alien standards of the town.

Every woman as she finished her letter found herself faced with the same problem as Bellag — there was no way of posting it unseen. By day it was impossible, and, in the few short hours of semi-darkness in the Hebridean summer, more than twenty women sneaking out to post formed a constant patrol in front of the pillar box as effective as a military guard.

At first each woman ignored the others, pretending that she was not there herself, but at last they acknowledged the facts and kept watch on a rota basis, passing the time in knitting, gossip and drinking tea. For a whole week the watch went on night after night from sunset to sunrise: each woman with a letter concealed on her person and no chance to post it. The occasion is remembered in the village tradition as the "week of the Pillar Box Wake," and it was a wake, for each of the women was sitting by the death bed of her own and her rivals hopes.

The women, however, did not keep watch alone.

Chapter XVI

"You would think for all the w-w-world they had b-b-bees after them," said Habakkuk, when the women fled from Bellag's on their letter writing spree.

"Aye," said Meesh, puffing at his old clay pipe, "it reminds me of the day the rat got up the captain's trousers."

"What happened then?" asked Cold Murdo, and they settled down for an evening of Meesh's yarns.

"It was off Cape Horn in a windjammer called the "Bride of Santa Fe," said Meesh. He paused as if making a strenous effort at precise recollection, "on a Wednesday morning, just after day-break."

"What course was she on?" asked Cold Murdo. Meesh told him. Questions followed on the state of the sea, the wind direction and force, the barometric pressure, and every other circumstance the old fishermen of Crobuie could think of to interrupt the narrative. It was all part of the ploy. If there had been any risk of putting Meesh off his stroke, the questions would have dried up immediately: they all wanted to hear the yarn, but in their own good time.

"It was all right until it reached his bellyband," said Meesh, when at last he was able to continue.

"It was a very experienced rat, an old salt of many voyages. A civil engineer couldn't have made a better job of tunnelling the ship's bulkheads, but the captain's bellyband was a new problem entirely: he couldn't climb over it, and he couldn't go under it. At least not without creating a considerable disturbance.

"The Captain was hitting the bottle. When the rat began to nibble he screamed and ran. 'Suicide' yelled the mate, and went after the captain. 'Murder!' yelled the bosun, and went after the mate. The rat ran, the captain ran, the mate ran, the bosun ran. Round and round the deck and up and down the rigging. You could hardly see their feet on the ladders they were going that fast, and the rat was meeting its own tail as it raced round the the captain's middle.

"The crew had been grumbling all voyage. They took the chance to mutiny and broach a cask of rum. There was the crew mad with drink shouting and singing on the deck, and the captain, the mate, the bosun and the rat, mad with lord knows what, yelling and screaming in the rigging.

"It was fair pandemonium," said Meesh with a chuckle, and an expansive wave of the hand to indicate the parallel with the madness which had overtaken the women.

"What happened then?" asked Cold Murdo, in accord with the unwritten convention that no story should be allowed to end until they had pumped the author dry. It was a great game trying to empty Meesh's barrel.

"They just went on running," said Meesh. "For all I know they may be running yet."

"I hardly thought you were old enough to have sailed in wind-jammers," said Willie with a sly look from under his eyebrows, modelled on Meesh's own.

"I wasn't," said Meesh.

"Then how do you know it happened?"

"A man told me, in a pub in Philadelphia." He paused then added with a wicked little grin, "It was a Wednesday morning, just after opening time."

"Did he tell you what the end of it was?" asked the Blacksmith.

"They were still running when he dived overboard and made his escape," said Meesh.

"How then did he know what caused it?" asked Willie triumphantly.

"It was himself that put the cheese in the captain's bellyband," said Meesh. Willie was generally worsted in his duels with Meesh but he knew there was no better training for a budding advocate.

"Do you think it's a rat that's bothering the women?" asked Cold Murdo, innocently.

"You better ask Willie that one," said Meesh. "He's been to the university."

"Women are not on the curriculum," said Willie with a laugh.

"Man," said Meesh sadly, "I don't know why they call it education. The one subject in the universe a man needs to understand, and it's not on the curriculum."

It was just then the Postmaster darted in like a man who had seen a ghost.

"She's writing a letter," he said in a panic. "What will I do if he takes her?"

Up to that point none of the men had seen any danger to himself in the women's capers about the advertisement, but in a moment the panic was general. No more terrible disaster could befall a man from Crobuie than to lose the sister, niece, or aunt, whose ministrations made life supportable.

Meesh alone was calm, which at the time they all thought greatly to his credit, except Willie, who knew the reason.

"I see your difficulty," said Meesh, with a thoughtful puff at his pipe. "She's inside the ring fence."

"She is that," said the Postmaster. Then with a look of great cunning he added, "I have the stamp in my pocket."

There was a murmur of approbation. He was a far-sighted man, the Postmaster; by keeping the official stamp on his own person he made sure that Katag could not put her letter directly into the mail. "I'll keep it under my pillow tonight," he added.

"That's not enough," said Meesh. "She can still use the pillar box."

"What do you suggest?" asked the Postmaster anxiously.

"Forbid her to write," said Meesh.

"Forbid?" asked the Postmaster, perplexed and terrified.

"Yes," said Meesh firmly, "forbid. If you don't know what it means, ask Willie — he's a walking encyclopedia. He knows everything in the universe that's no use to anyone."

"I cannot forbid her," said the Postmaster timidly.

Again there was a murmur of approbation. None of them would dare forbid their womenfolk. Meesh was asking too much.

"Well," said Meesh gaily, "Cold Murdo will help you."

Cold Murdo put on his bonnet and made for the door. "I cannot manage my own," he said, "let alone tackle another man's."

"It's a poor spirit," said Meesh, "if a man won't smoke a pipe for a friend."

"What do you mean?" asked Cold Murdo.

"She daren't post when the shop is shut," said Meesh. "The other women will see to that. Her only chance is to sneak it in when the shop is open, and himself is out. Now if Cold Murdo was sitting on a boll of meal in the corner of the shop, smoking his pipe, what chance would she have?"

"I'm greatly indebted to you," said the Postmaster, with dignity and the others joined in applauding Meesh's stratagem. In a few minutes a rota was drawn up so that from opening time to closing time there was at least one man present in the shop, to safeguard against the possibility of the Postmaster being called away leaving Katag in control of the field.

So the Pillar Box wake went on by day as by night. In fact it might be going yet but for a circumstance even Meesh himself had not foreseen.

It took dynamite to establish a new habit in Crobuie, so set in their ways had the ancients become, but once a new routine was adopted, it became a habit over-night. Willie could foresee that, many years on, when he was old and decrepit himself, the imperishable bodachs and cailleahs in Crobuie would still mount guard on the village Post Office. The day might even come when Winter assured them that the custom had its origin in the Crimean war, and they believed him, because no one remembered anything to the contrary.

But Willie's dream was shattered by the unexpected arrival of a little horse-faced man in Harris Tweed, carrying a black brief case with the letter M.F. and a crown embossed in gold.

Chapter XVII

It was the time of the changing of the guard. The Postmaster was taking down the shutters, and preparing for the morning's business. Katag was hovering in the background, watching her chance, like a hungry sparrow trying to share a meal with the cat. The rest of the women were gathered in a sleepy, dispirited group at the end of their night-long vigil, waiting for the men to take over. The fact that the men were fresh, amiable and talkative, after a comfortable night in bed, had much the same effect as a thunder-storm on a jug of milk — it made them exceedingly sour.

The men made as much cheerful noise as possible: life had no greater joy to offer them than the sight of the women slinking home each morning after what was for each of them a night of frustration and defeat. Only one man was due for rota duty at a time, and the men of Crobuie were not addicted to early rising, but in the week of the wake the first man on each day could count on the company of every male in the village.

"It's a terrible affliction that's come on Crobuie," said Meesh with unction.

"It is that," said the Blacksmith, with the faintest hint of a smile. "They've never been worse."

"I was going down the croft yesterday to do a bit of hoeing," said Cold Murdo. "I just happened to be whistling to myself with the high spirits. Chrissie Macluggage was going down the other side of the fence to feed the hens, and she flung the basin at me."

"The mess for the hens was still in it," he added.

"What were you whistling?" asked Meesh.

"Ho ro my nut brown maiden," said Cold Murdo solemnly.

"That's dangerous," said Meesh. "It's worse than a red rag to a bull. Never sing that if there's more than three within earshot. It's bad enough having a wake in the village without having a death."

The two groups met, the men with effusive good mornings, the women with silence and black looks. Meesh was considering how to stir the antagonism into active life when he saw a strange figure on the sky-line. He watched it with a seaman's eye for a few moments, trying to make out the rig and the course of the strange vessel. At last he spoke.

"I don't like the cut of his jib," he said emphatically.

They all looked.

"Who is it?" asked the Blacksmith.

"That's what I want to know," said Meesh. "He didn't grow out of the heather."

"Perhaps it's a hiker with a tent," suggested the Postmaster, who joined them to inspect the phenomenon. Any visitor to Crobuie was an event but a stranger at daybreak was against the course of nature.

"It's not a hiker," said Meesh, who by this time had his telescope poised against the Post Office door. "His boots are clean. He shaved this morning."

"You mean?" asked the Postmaster anxiously.

"I do that," said Meesh. "There's no where else."

The men of Crobuie were glum as they tried to digest the news that the stranger approaching the village must have spent the night with Finch.

"They've sacked Finch!" suggested the Blacksmith at last. "It's a new gamekeeper."

Meesh gave him a scornful look.

"He's the very picture of a gamekeeper," he said, sarcastically. "Just look at his stride."

The Blacksmith muttered something in reply, but he had to admit the justice of the rebuke. The stranger was daintly picking his steps between the puddles like a nervous woman on stepping stones with the river in spate.

"It's bad, bad, bad," said Meesh. "I'm afraid the weather's breaking."

By this time the women had turned back to join them. Sleepy though they were, the appearance of a strange man in Crobuie startled them into alertness.

"Meesh is worried," said Maggie Moogish, sharply.

"With good reason," he said solemnly.

Meesh was deeply troubled, but he was not above turning it to account.

"Who is it?" asked Chrissie Bell Macluggage.

"I think it's himself," said Meesh slowly. "Coming to have a look."

"What do you mean?" demanded Maggie.

"Figure it out for yourself," said Meesh. "It's more than a week since he advertised, and he hasn't had a single reply."

In a moment the women were broad awake, tidying their clothes, patting their hair in place. They were straining at the leash, but none of them had the effrontery to accost the stranger openly. Not even Maggie.

"Aye," said Meesh with a solemn shake of the head. "It's an awful affliction to be tethered just out of reach of the corn."

"Mind your own business," snapped Maggie.

"It's early in the year for wasps," said Cold Murdo, brushing an imaginery insult from his face, but looking straight at his niece.

"Some folk have bees in their bonnets all the year round," said Maggie, and the women murmured their agreement. They were tired of being baited.

Meesh seemed on the point of saying something really explosive, and the men watched him expectantly. The women, however, had their eyes fixed on the stranger. Suddenly he missed his footing on a bit of shingle, staggered drunkenly across the road, and sat with a splash in a huge puddle of peaty brown water.

It was the opportunity the women were waiting for. Like runners at the starter's gun, they dashed to the rescue. Helter skelter up the slope from the Post Office, slithering on the muddy ground. Most of them jumped the ditch, and those that couldn't splashed through it regardless. Even the barbed wire fence did not dismay them.

"Man," said Meesh, "you would think they dressed ship for the occasion." He pointed to strips of cloth like pennants and streamers in the breeze, where the women had forced their way between the strands.

"They'll be busy with the needles in Crobuie tonight," said Cold Murdo. His heart shrank at the prospect of buying his niece a new skirt.

"There's more than skirts needing patching," said Meesh darkly. The visit of a stranger with a brief case to Crobuie had a sinister significance.

"I wonder who it really is?" asked the Postmaster gloomily.

Meesh pulled himself together and smiled. "I haven't an earthly," he said, "but he'll be needing a dry pair of pants." He looked round the group quizzically as if measuring them for size. "I think it'll have to be my own," he said, making for home.

"You're far too big," said Cold Murdo. "Your trousers would make him a tent."

"Precisely," said Meesh with a chuckle.

Chapter XVIII

"Finch didn't waste much time," said Meesh as he rummaged among the old clothes in the kist.

"How do you know it's Finch?" challenged Willie. "You're jumping to conclusions."

"What else could M.F. stand for?" asked Meesh.

"It could be Ministry of Food," said Willie, with an indulgent smile.

"Precisely," said Meesh. "It was a great mistake not asking Finch to the barbecue."

"He's got you on the run this time," said Willie.

"You think so?" asked Meesh. As a budding lawyer Willie should know.

"I don't see how you can get out of it," said Willie. "There's illicit slaughter for one thing. A rationing offence for another. The Missionary's in it, too. In fact you're all in it, and I'm in it with you."

"It's not the fine. It's not even the prison," said Meesh despondently. "It's the grin on Finch's face."

"I'll do what I can," said Willie. "I know a lawyer who'll appear for us cheap."

"It's not a lawyer we need, it's a lifebelt," said Meesh. Willie had never seen him in the dumps before.

"Cheer up, Meesh," he said. "We won't let you drown."

"Honesty is a terrible burden at a time like this," said Meesh. "Like swimming in heavy boots. Man if we weren't so bad for telling the truth, we could wriggle out of it in no time."

"Don't tell me you've a conscience, Meesh, I just won't believe it," said Willie, seriously, but not unkindly.

"Conscience?" said Meesh. "It's worse than a hump or a wooden leg. It's a terrible disability for a man to have when he's in trouble. Crobuie is rotten with it."

Willie would have put it differently, but he could see what Meesh was driving at. The Missionary was liable to blurt the whole story out as soon as the snooper from the Ministry went to work on him.

"There's the women, too," said Meesh. "Leaky pans the lot of them. We're in a bad way."

"You have only yourself to blame for the women," said Willie. He was getting quite short with Meesh. He was in trouble too; his career might be affected if he had a prosecution against him, but Meesh was moaning, as if the whole burden fell on him. "I told you not to meddle," he said. "You wouldn't listen to me, and a fine mess you've made of it."

Meesh smiled, a broad, warm-hearted smile, like a harvest moon.

"Willie, Willie, Willie," he said affably. "It's well seen you've never played poker."

"You've played it once too often," said Willie. He was now the despondent one, while Meesh was chuckling to himself like a hen that's laid an egg. He held up a pair of trousers for Willie's inspection. They were grotesquely misshapen. They would have looked ridiculous on Meesh himself, but the prim little horse-faced man would be lost in them like a bird beneath a table-cloth.

"I think this will do," he said with deep satisfaction.

"Leave well alone," said Willie desperately, but Meesh was gone. Through the half open door Willie could hear him extolling the virtues of the trousers to the Ministry official. "Aye, man," said Meesh. "It's a fine pair of pants: you could carry the wife and family with you like a kangaroo."

The horse-faced man looked at the trousers with disgust. He disliked the idea of putting on any stranger's clothes, let alone thick kersey, seven sizes too big for him. He hesitated, then took the plunge. His own clothes were soaking; the alternative was to shiver in nakedness until they dried.

"Thank you," he said without much conviction, and began to dress like a timid bather inveigled into having a dip on a frosty February morning. Meesh hurried in with the wet clothes, grinning happily.

"Incommunicado!" he said to Willie, as he arranged the clothes in front of the fire. "That's what the Spaniards say."

"Meaning?" asked Willie without much enthusiasm.

"We've got to keep him from talking to the women."

"That won't be easy," said Willie, and on the words Bellag bounced in, glowing with the exertion of hurrying through the village with an ashet in her arms. Through the cloth which covered it Willie could see the contours of a fine fat chicken. Hot at her heels came Maggie Moogish carrying an even larger dish piled high with home-baked scones. They glowered at each other. Katag and Chrissie Macluggage elbowed viciously when they met in the doorway a few seconds later, hurrying in with their tribute. In a short time the room was full of women, with baskets, plates or bags, and the air was like a bake-house when the batch comes hot from the oven.

"They're going to fatten him for the kill," said Meesh in a whisper to Willie.

"We're for the kill," said Willie. "He'll have the whole story in half an hour."

"I've seen it scores of times in Salt Lake City," said Meesh, raising his voice slightly, so that some of the women round about could just hear him if they listened closely.

"Seen what?" asked Willie.

"The sign," said Meesh.

"Sign?" asked Willie, puzzled.

"M.F.," said Meesh.

"I've read about it," said Willie, taking the cue. Meesh was delighted at his pupil's aptness. "I believe it stands for Mormon Fraternity."

"That's right," said Meesh. "The crown is the symbol of man's supremacy. They keep the women there." He made an expressive gesture with his thumb.

"How many wives can they have?" asked Willie, also raising his voice ever so slightly.

"There's no limit," said Meesh. "Ten's a fair average."

"It's worse than slavery," said Willie.

"Ugly," said Meesh. "You never saw the like of them."

"The women?" asked Willie.

"No, the men," said Meesh. "Some of them have two heads, but the most of them have no head at all, at least nothing you could call a head. It scunners you to look at them."

"That's funny," said Willie. "He's a bit like a horse, but I wouldn't call him a bad looker."

"That's the point," said Meesh. "They never go themselves: they know they haven't a chance. They always a hire a nice young man to do the booking for them. Once you've signed the paper there's no escape. You see some of the loveliest women married to the ugliest men. That is if you call it married, when you're only one of ten."

"I've warned, Annie," he added. "She's making him a cup of tea, from the goodness of her heart, but as soon as he drinks it — . . ." Meesh made a gesture with his hands as if driving a cow from the crops.

"Where has everyone gone?" asked Annie bustling in.

"That's odd," said Meesh looking round in well feigned astonishment, "The room was full a moment ago."

"The whole village was here," said Willie. "And I didn't even see them go."

"There's no accounting for women," said Meesh sadly. "They're on the fidget all day long."

"Did you tell them who he is?" asked Annie.

"I dropped a hint," said Meesh.

Annie hurried out again, to get food for the stranger.

"Which did you tell her?" asked Willie. "Mormon or Ministry?"

"I told her the truth," said Meesh. "You can't go up Annie's sleeve."

"Did you ever try blowing on a snowball to see how quickly you can melt it?" he added, looking round at the empty room. Willie laughed.

"That's one crisis over," he said. "But what about the information he has already?"

"That's more difficult," said Meesh. "But not impossible."

"What are you planning?" asked Willie with a smile.

"They're drying too quickly," said Meesh irrelevantly. He took the stranger's trousers out and dipped them in the water butt.

"When they're dry," he said, "you can take him back to Finch."

"Why don't you take him yourself?" asked Willie.

"It's an odd thing," said Meesh, "but I have a great urge to go poaching."

"I thought all the fun was out of it," said Willie.

"There's poaching and poaching," said Meesh mysteriously.

Willie would have pursued the theme, but just then the stranger came shuffling in, as if his feet were tied in a sack. The sleeves flapped as he walked, and the jacket dangled half way down his calves like an ill-fitting overcoat. Willie had never seen such a scarecrow. He was terrified Meesh would whisper some comment, and make him laugh.

But Meesh greeting the stranger warmly, helped him to a seat by the fire and plied him with hot tea and buttered scones heaped high with crowdie. It was years since the stranger had eaten such wholesome, satisfying food.

When the meal was over, Meesh handed him a cigarette, lit the old clay pipe, and entertained him by the hour with tale after tale of his seafaring days. In a short time the horse-faced man forgot his embarrassment. Meesh was the most interesting and affable character he had ever met.

A column of steam from the stranger's clothes rose briskly in the glow of the fire, mingling with the blue smoke from the peats.

By nightfall they were dry.

When the stranger had taken a cordial farewell of Meesh and Annie, Willie led him through the village to Finch's cottage.

Meesh watched them go, and when the dusk had swallowed them, he slipped quietly into the night himself, carrying a torch, a spade and a long sharp knife.

Chapter XIX

The offical from the Ministry was perturbed when, later in the evening, he learned from Finch that Meesh was the principal culprit in the breach of regulations he had come to investigate. In spite of the ill-fitting trousers, he had taken a liking to Meesh, and had no wish to get him into trouble.

To begin with, the vindictiveness with which Finch spoke of the Crobuie folk prejudiced him in their favour. He felt there was malice behind it, and discounted the tales of thievery on the river and violence on the hill.

"They're not a bad lot really, are they now?" he asked.

"Bad?" said Finch. "They would steal the feathers from an angel's wings, and ask a tip for their trouble."

"Oh, come, come," said the official, mildly protesting.

"I know them," said Finch aggressively. "I've suffered them too damn long for my comfort. Your hair would stand on end, if I told you some of the things they do."

Finch was not an imaginative man, and the libels on Crobuie, which he coughed up in his rancour, were quite incredible, but his account of the mauling he had received from the women was so circumstantial, and was vouched by so much real evidence of violence on his person, that the official was finally convinced, and accepted the embellishments as well.

"Look at the fool he made of yourself, dressing you in these ridiculous trousers," said Finch, who had heard some of the villagers laughing over Meesh's latest prank. It was a new idea to the official that the trousers had been chosen deliberately as an assault on his dignity. He saw in a flash that Meesh was a cunning rogue and hypocrite: Crobuie a hot-bed of vice. Before he retired for the night, he wrote a strong report in which the events of the barbecue were set out in detail, and the whole affair given a sinister implication which it did not really have. "The people of Crobuie are lawless and defiant," he concluded. "Regulations mean nothing to them."

A wave of horror surged through the Ministry, mounting as it went, like a tide race funnelling through a strait, and spilling over sunken reefs in a white fury. The rebellion in Crobuie terrified and angered them. It struck at the very foundations of their universe. To the Hindu the cow is sacred: to the bureaucrat, the book of rules.

"Anarchy," muttered one. "The termites are at work," muttered another, and, in an apocalyptic vision, all who heard him could see the crofters of Crobuie bring the empire tottering to ruin by gnawing at the structure from within.

Few of the officials had been further north than the Trossachs. Their knowledge of the Hebrides consisted of half-remembered snatches of

Scottish history in its bloodiest and most irrational moments, and such insight into the folkways as could be gathered from the music halls, Sunday papers and comic postcards. "They carry dirks in their stockings," one official told his secretary, and she wondered at the daring of the man who dealt with such dangerous monsters even by intra-departmental minute.

If Crobuie had been in Central Africa (as some of them at first supposed) a punitive expedition would have been sent to fire the thatch, and smoke the rebels out, but it was discovered in time that the village was technically part of the United Kingdom.

"How on earth did that come about?" asked the Minister of Food bleakly. It was a shock to discover that Hebrideans are white, human and British.

Since it was out of the question to use the violent methods which would have been appropriate for a civilised nation dealing with an uncivilised, the Ministry decided to prosecute the whole male population of the village, (except, of course, Finch).

The Postmaster was terrified when the summonses arrived. They had to lie in the office overnight, awaiting the morning delivery. He handled them like dynamite, and slept as uneasily as if he suspected an assassin under the bed. It would have eased his mind to discuss the situation with Meesh but, not even in his extremity, would he disclose the contents of the mail. By the time he had delivered all the summonses most of the men were already with Meesh holding a council of war.

In ordinary circumstances the women of Crobuie would have been in mourning. It was a dreadful calamity to be summoned to court even as a witness. But so great was the change which Meesh had worked on the village, the women were jubilant.

"I hope they get sixty days breaking stones," said Maggie Moogish viciously.

"It'll be a quiet village without them right enough," said Bellag complacently.

Katag said nothing: she hurried home to pack her brother's bag, as if to speed him on his way. She had a strange idea how he would live, if he was gaoled, for, with sisterly solicitude, she packed him all the comforts she could think of, even his rainbow dressing gown with the tasselled belt, which was the wonder and the envy of the village. "It'll be a rest to get rid of him," she told herself gaily. She was quite sure she could run the Post Office more efficiently without him, and probably she was right. Moreover it would give her an opportunity to post her letter.

"I had nothing to do with it," said the Missionary frantically as he hurried into Meesh's. "It was your sheep."

"Oh no," said Meesh. "It was yours."

"Morally, it was yours," said the Missionary. "You told me that yourself."

"Unfortunately," said Meesh. "The law has no morals. Legally the sheep was yours."

"If it was, you stole it," said the Missionary. "I'll charge the lot of you with theft."

"You ate your own good share of it," said Meesh.

"And said the grace," added Cold Murdo.

"Under duress," protested the Missionary, who now and then liked to use a big word no one knew the meaning of — least of all himself.

"Under nothing," said the Blacksmith, vindictively. "It was down on the machair in the open air."

"With Finch looking on," said Cold Murdo. "The damned little ferret."

"It's a shocking state of affairs when the law takes the word of a gamekeeper," said Meesh. "It's a poor profession you're going into, Willie."

"In a case like this the evidence of one witness is not enough," said Willie.

The Blacksmith threw his hat in the air and shouted "hurrah."

"Not so fast," cautioned Willie. "There's circumstantial evidence. I saw them myself down at the machair. The mark of the fire was still quite clear, and the bones were still there where we buried them. They dug them up and took them away."

"And the head with my earmarks on it," said the Missionary, dolefully.

"That's it," said Willie. "You can't argue with that sort of evidence."

"Will they send us to gaol?" asked the Missionary.

"I don't think so, but they'll probably fine us severely. After all it was a pretty blatant offence," said Willie.

"It was our own sheep," said the Blacksmith.

"Yes," said Willie, "But it's their law."

The crofters couldn't see what the law had to do with them eating their own sheep. Even when Willie pointed out that they were getting a subsidy from the government for rearing their sheep they were not convinced. A subsidy was manna from heaven, something the good Lord intended them to enjoy, but that the subsidy should be subject to inconvenient rules was altogether wrong.

"It's a long way to the Sheriff Court," said Meesh at last, "and we're all old men. I think we should wait until they come for us."

Willie dissented. He didn't see the sense of prolonging the agony, and annoying the Sheriff but the others agreed with Meesh. If the law wanted them, the law could come for them.

The failure of the crofters to answer the summons, created a problem for the authorities. The simultaneous arrest of more than twenty people was unheard of in the Highlands since the crofting riots in the middle of the 19th century, or at least since the trouble over the union of the churches. There weren't twenty policemen in the whole of the Hebrides, even if they could all be spared for this important task. Even if there had been policemen, there was no road to Crobuie that a black maria could run on, and no black maria, even if there had been a road.

It was finally decided to send a single policeman on foot to reason with them. The people of Crobuie were normally open to reason, but unfortunately, when the policeman arrived, they were all at a fank, in a remote part of the moor, even the Postmaster who had never been at a fank since he became a government official: even Winter who had to be carried in a creel by the others because he couldn't walk so far. The women had no idea how long the fank would last, because a fank had never been held in that part of the moor before, and there were as many different ideas of where exactly it was as there were women in the village. They were quite happy to see the men getting into trouble with the law, but it was contrary to the ethics of Crobuie to help a policeman even in such a righteous cause. Bowls of milk, plates of broth, mealy puddings, yes, but information, no!

There was no telephonic communication between Crobuie and the outside world. In the 1914-18 war a telephone line had been erected at fabulous cost to serve the needs of a coastguard station set up by the Admiralty, but, when the war was over, the wire was sold to a scrap merchant to save the nation from bankruptcy, and the poles were left staggering drunkenly across the moor, of no service even as signposts because they took the shortest route, straight through the wettest part of the bog.

The policeman was in a quandary. There was no sign of the men coming back from the fank, even as darkness fell, and there was no means of getting in touch with headquarters for fresh instructions. However, the food was good, and he decided to stay the night, although for reasons of discretion, both personal and official, he slept in Finch's cottage, rather than in the homes where he had dined and supped.

The sea air is soporific, especially after a hearty Crobuie supper, and the policeman woke in the morning to find that the men had been home for the night, but had left for another fank. Borrowing Finch's telescope he went in search of them. It was late in the day before he even sighted them, and just as he got them focussed in the glass the men broke up into small groups and disappeared further into the hills, as if rounding up strays. But oddly, he noticed, they had neither sheep nor dogs. He returned to Finch weary and exasperated.

Next morning he was up betimes, but it was obvious that the men had been even earlier, at least there was no sign of life in the village. With Finch to reinforce him, the policeman set off in pursuit. It was a warm day and the heavy serge uniform was most uncomfortable, but he plodded gamely on: hour after hour, jumping gullies in the moor, splashing through boggy patches, tripping and stumbling on the gnarled roots of the heather. From daybreak to nightfall he saw no sign of man or dog.

It was only when he got back to the village he discovered that the men had been at home all day, resting in their beds. At first he was furious, but, when he considered the matter reasonably and honestly, he had to admit that no one told him in the morning that the men had gone, although somehow that impression seemed implicit in the very walk and bearing of the women. There was nothing he could do that night, even when he made the discovery: he was too tired to move another step, and in any event, as he and Finch returned from one direction, the men of Crobuie had been setting off in another to have their fank, apparently by moonlight.

In the morning, the policeman left for home. It was a good five miles to the nearest bus route, and he took the short cut across the moor, rather than venture his limbs on the remnants of the Crobuie road, now like a dried-out river bed with erosion and neglect.

That was unfortunate because the Procurator Fiscal, coming in search of him, stuck to the road, such as it was. The Fiscal was accompanied by a posse of armed policeman borrowed from the mainland.

He was new to the Isles, and, judging the situation in the light of his city experience, he made a most regrettable misjudgement — he failed to realise that in Crobuie even authority must conform to the pace of the community; and, when his policeman did not return, he decided forthwith that he had been slashed with a razor and left dying in a ditch.

The Chief Constable, who was an islander himself, tried to disabuse the Fiscal's mind, but that energetic busybody was quite persuaded he had a murder on his hands, and, filled with his own importance, he arranged for a retinue of efficient mainland officers to be flown to the isles. Immediately the plane touched down they set out for Crobuie in two buses, with a large supply of handcuffs borrowed here and there throughout Scotland, to take the insurgents to gaol.

When they had gone by bus as far as it was possible for a vehicle to go, the column halted. The men were drawn up in military fashion, and harangued by the Fiscal on the dangerous operation they were about to engage in, and the need for prompt and valiant action. The men were amused, because most of them were Highlanders and suffered in some small measure from the Crobuie-complex.

They were still more amused when they came in sight of the village and saw that it was en fete to receive them. Stretched across between Maggie's barn and the Missionary's byre was a banner with the legend, ''Ceud Mile Failte'' — ''a hundred thousand welcomes.'' For want of real bunting, Meesh had used a strip torn from an old blanket, and the words were painted on with tar, but it was obvious from the arrangements made to receive the force that the welcome was genuine. Nothing so exciting as the arrival of thirty six policemen had happened in Crobuie for upwards of eighty years, and in every house in the village tables were spread for the guests. It was with difficulty Willie dissuaded Meesh from garlanding the Fiscal in the fashion he had seen in the South Sea Islands.

That worthy official suspected a trap. Declined all hospitality. Ordered the captives to be handcuffed forthwith, and marched to the waiting buses.

''Man,'' said Meesh affably, ''It's an awful pity you're using these things — I arranged a piper to head the procession.''

The handcuffs made piping out of the question, but it takes more than handcuffs to stifle a Gaelic song. From Crobuie to the gates of the gaol, Meesh and his companions enlivened the way with love songs, labour songs, laments, and even psalms, until the poor Fiscal was nearly crazy with the din, and furious at the affront to his own dignity. It made it worse that some of the policemen were so far carried away as to hum the catchier tunes, and even tap the floor of the bus in time to the music.

"Barbarians!" spluttered the Fiscal, as he stepped down from the bus to superintend the incarceration of twenty-three people in a gaol designed for six.

His temper was not improved by the fact that he could not understand how Meesh knew the police were coming. He suspected a quisling in the camp, being a firm disbeliever in the second sight.

Chapter XX

"I wonder will they let us out for the funeral?" asked Meesh reflectively, as they crowded into the cell.

"Funeral?" echoed the Missionary timidly.

"Aye," said Meesh. "It's a solemn thought that a man can survive the snows of the Crimea only to die of suffocation in a prison cell."

Willie took the point. "I think we should make a formal protest," he said. "They have no right to pack us in like this. It's injurious to health."

Quickly Willie drafted a petition, and wisely Meesh made no suggestions. He realised that it was a matter which Willie was better qualified to deal with by himself.

Even at the best of times Winter seemed frailer than he really was, but by the time the prison doctor arrived to make an inspection, he looked more like death than death itself. His condition was partly due to genuine distress, for the cell was shockingly over-crowded, partly it was auto-suggestion, and partly it was the application of a little flour from a prison loaf which Meesh thoughtfully rubbed into the old man's cheeks.

The prison doctor was one of the general practitioners of the town. He was called on so seldom in his official capacity that he had forgotten he held the office until the police took him from more urgent duties to make his report. He was not very pleased at the interruption of his routine, and he took it out on the Fiscal. His report was blunt almost to savagery.

In a panic the Fiscal inspected all public buildings in the town — hospitals, schools, hotels, even the Freemason's hall and the Fish Market — but he decided that none of them was sufficiently lockfast to serve as a temporary prison for such dangerous criminals as the rebellious crofters from Crobuie. Reluctantly he decided to fly the younger and fitter prisoners to gaol in Inverness and Aberdeen.

"Man," said Meesh to Willie, as the plane took off, "I had no idea you got a free flight to Aberdeen as discount on a half-crown advertisement."

"What was that about advertisement?" asked Cold Murdo sharply. Willie felt sure he was beginning to suspect that Meesh had been behind it all.

"I was just saying that Katag will be able to reply to the advertisement," said Meesh, unabashed. "The Postmaster isn't there to stop her," he added in explanation.

Cold Murdo took the bait.

"Aye," he said. "She's inside the ring fence." He had no idea that he was merely quoting Meesh.

Fortunately the Postmaster was not in the plane with them. He might have jumped out with anxiety, if he heard the men discuss the peril he was in, and the shock he would get when he was finally released from gaol, and found a stranger married to Katag, and installed behind the Office counter. Not even a film star or a cabinet minister, most of them felt sure, would pass up the opportunity of being Postmaster in Crobuie. It was a position of great dignity and trust. It was also lucrative — by Crobuie standards.

Having flown the prisoners to the mainland, it was necessary to fly them back again to face their trial. This shuttling back and fore of aeroplanes and policemen aroused the interest of the press, and there was a quite unusual array of journalists in court when the men of Crobuie appeared to plead.

"Not guilty," said Meesh, with sailor-like smartness. "Not guilty," said Willie in an embarrassed whisper. "Not g-g-g-guilty," stammered Habakkuk. And so it went, down the line, to old Winter himself, whose high pitched treble wailed like a banshee through the court-room. Meesh intimated that they would conduct their own defence.

The Sheriff, a lean, shrivelled man, like a desiccated sparrow, ancient, a little wandered, and stone deaf, tried to persuade them to engage a solicitor, when the Sheriff Clerk, with much bellowing, and a desperate resort to sign language, had at length explained the situation to him.

Willie would have liked to engage a solicitor, and argued the point heatedly with Meesh for days on end, but Meesh was adamant, and he talked the others into his way of thinking. "The less we have to do with lawyers the better," he said. "It's a lawyer that got us into this jam."

"Yes," said Willie, "and it's only a lawyer that can get us out of it."

"I would sooner a sheep's head than a lawyer's any day," said Meesh cryptically.

"This is a serious matter," replied Willie, appealing urgently to the rest of the crowd.

"That's why," said Meesh.

The trial was over quickly. The Fiscal, brisk and efficient, presented his evidence with despatch. The police told the court of the arrest, and formally identified the accused. The Ministry's Inspector told how he visited Crobuie and found a sheep's head at the site of the fire. The sheep's head was produced. It was sealed, labelled, signed and counter-signed by the Ministry Official, Finch and the Police Inspector. There could be no doubt that it was the veritable head found at the scene of the crime.

It smelt offensively, despite the fact that the Fiscal had stored it in his own refrigerator with the Sunday joint, and once it had been identified, the Sheriff suggested that it be removed to the cells. At that stage it did not look as if it would be required again: none of the accused had any questions for witnesses, they just sat staring stolidly in front of them as if they had no interest whatsoever in the events about them.

When Finch took the stand he avoided even a glance in the direction of the dock: he was afraid a smile of triumph might break across his face. He had waited long to see Meesh sitting there.

Like a good game-keeper, he gave his evidence crisply, accurately, and with an eye for significant detail. He had it all: the preparation of the grid-iron for the barbecue, the quarrel over the sheep, the round up of the Missionary's ewe, and the arrival of the women at the feast.

"Man, I didn't think there was that much poetry in him," said Meesh with genuine admiration, as Finch described, in almost lyrical terms, the smell of roasting mutton which spread across Crobuie drawing the women, as if hypnotised, to the barbecue.

Willie made no reply. He was too worried about his own predicament for aesthetic appreciation of the game-keeper's language. But everyone else in Court except the Sheriff, who hadn't heard a word, began to salivate profusely.

"Do any of you wish to ask questions of this witness?" asked the Sheriff when the Fiscal had completed his examination. This time Meesh rose briskly in his place.

"It's an evil thing spite?" he began.

"It is that," said Finch with an almost genial smile.

"It's bad, bad, when a man frames-up his neighbour?"

"It is that," agreed Finch. He felt that his triumph was complete when Meesh went floundering about in such irrelevancies.

"It was one of the Missionary's sheep?" asked Meesh.

"It was," said Finch. "His best."

"I think I would like to see the head again," said Meesh to no one in particular. The Sheriff, the Sheriff Clerk, the Fiscal, the police — and although they had no voice in it — the public — were all reluctant to see the stinking horror brought back to Court, but Meesh insisted on his rights.

The head was preceded by the smell. Through long corridors in the cavernous depths below the court room, and up the long stone stair, it wafted. Before the head had even left the cell, noses were twitching apprehensively. The smell was as strident, as all pervasive, as insistent, as a pipe band in a small room, but while one can shut the ears to an offensive sound, one cannot stop breathing and live.

Meesh looked stolidly in front of him, although even he felt sick, and when at last the head arrived, he took it in his hands, almost lovingly, and held it up for Finch to see.

"You know the Missionary's earmarks?" he asked.

"I do," said Finch, turning his head away from the smell.

"Whose earmarks are those?" asked Meesh quietly, thrusting the head still closer to Finch's nose.

With an effort Finch forced himself to bend over and examine the ears.

"I'm waiting," said Meesh, with a faint edge of impatience in his voice, but Finch made no reply.

"I don't see the relevancy of this," interrupted the Fiscal.

"Neither do I," said the Sheriff, who hadn't heard a word, but wished to be rid of the smell.

"I'm still waiting for an answer," said Meesh.

Finch lost control. "You're a damned twister," he yelled, and thumped the witness-box in his rage.

"That's no language to use before his Lordship," said Meesh reprovingly. Finch swore again.

"Whose ear-marks are those?" asked Meesh insistently.

"Well you know," shouted Finch.

"Maybe I do," said Meesh, "But his Lordship doesn't."

By this time the Sheriff was aware that something had gone wrong, although the angry voices made no more sense than the murmur of bees on a sunny afternoon. He foresaw that the offensive head might be with him for quite a long time if the deadlock was not broken quickly. "Answer the question," he snapped.

Finch, with a thin sibilant hiss, like a deflating tyre, said weakly, "They're mine."

Meesh sat down. His face was inscrutable, but Willie could sense that he was laughing deep within. The Fiscal was purple with indignation, at Meesh for out-witting him, and at Finch for leading him into such a silly trap.

"This alters the whole case, my lord," he said petulantly. "I don't think I need go any further."

The Sheriff blinked. It was not often the Fiscal was so brief in his address to the Court, but no doubt, thought his Lordship, it was a clear-cut case.

"Do any of you wish to say anything in your own defence?" he asked the accused, looking round apprehensively. The prospect of more than twenty speeches appalled him. Why had the fools not engaged a lawyer?

"I understood the Fiscal to say that he was dropping the charge," said Meesh.

"That is so," snapped the Fiscal, sweeping his papers together, and gathering his gown about him, ready to leave.

"This is a bad, bad case," began his Lordship. The Fiscal knew that he had heard nothing, and was going to convict. He was tempted to let him go on, but in spite of his rage, professional integrity — and the fear of an appeal — forbade it.

"I wish to drop the case," he bellowed with his cupped hands held near the Sheriff's ear. "I have insufficient evidence."

The Sheriff grunted his dis-satisfaction. He was annoyed at losing the chance of delivering the harangue he had rehearsed the night before on the evils of mass disobedience to the law. Accustomed as he was to the delights of the city, he resented his exile in a remote part of the Highlands, where the people spoke an uncouth language of their own. He regarded the crofters as inferior creatures to be stamped on at every opportunity like insects under a stone.

The reporters shot out from the court like rockets. There were only one trunk line, and it was a mad scramble to get the messages through. The few members of the public who had been present sauntered out more leisurely, discussing the odd turn of events.

"You're a genius, Meesh, a real genius," said Willie, grasping the old salt's hand, as they left the court together. The other accused followed them, not quite sure whether they were on their way to the cells, or home to Crobuie.

"How much did he say the fine was?" asked the Postmaster tugging at Willie's sleeve.

"They'll rope us to the guns in the snow," said Winter, on the verge of tears, his mind wandering back to tales he had heard of field punishment in the Crimea.

The Missionary lingered behind the others in the empty Court room to put up a silent prayer. It was just possible that he was going to the gallows — he was not quite sure.

"Now," said Willie to Meesh. "How did you do it?"

"Well," said Meesh, "if he was as good a shepherd as he is a game-keeper, he wouldn't have left that wedder to drown."

"I see," said Willie. "You exchanged the heads?"

"It's wonderful what a man can do with a spade when he's hard put to it," said Meesh, a little smugly.

Chapter XXI

"That was a good plate of porridge," said Meesh, licking the spoon until it shone. The night drive and the long morning walk, after prison fare, had given him such an appetite as he had not known for years.

"There's a letter on the mantlepiece," said Annie frigidly. She had waited until he was fortified with food before breaking the news. Letters were ominous in Crobuie, for no one had any occasion to write to the dying village.

"It's from the newspaper office," added Annie, and there was menace in her voice.

Inwardly Meesh cursed the fools who were so pleased with the name of their paper that they plastered it all over the envelope.

He knew it was Katag's reply to the advertisement. There was nothing in life he wanted more than to read it over quietly with Willie, but if he opened it, Annie would see it by hook or crook. Without a word, he tossed the un-opened letter in the fire.

"Why did you do that, you fool?" demanded Annie.

"There's no point in wasting my eyesight — I know what's in it," said Meesh unmoved.

Annie singed her fingers as she tried to rescue the blazing fragments. Quick though she had been, she retrieved nothing of significance: Meesh was too careful with his aim.

"I know what was in it too," said Annie, tartly, as she rubbed butter on her burnt thumb.

"I doubt it," said Meesh, but he feared the worst, for Annie's powers of divination were not unlike his own. For one horrible moment, he wondered whether she had steamed the envelope open, but he knew she would not stoop to that, and if she had stooped to it, she would not have thrust her fingers into the fire.

"I'll find out for sure, sooner or later," said Annie, and Meesh had an uncomfortable feeling that she would.

"It had to do with the case," he said, stretching the truth but only, he assured himself, within permissible limits.

"If it had, you would have read it," said Annie. "You're as pleased about that case as a cat with two tails."

Meesh said nothing, but, after a few moments' silence Annie added, darkly, "one of these days you'll get into a corner you can't get out of."

Again Meesh felt that there was a bite in the words. He was glad when Willie's arrival created a diversion. "I think we'll go for a walk through the village," he said.

"Have you not had enough walking for a day," said Willie, who was quite tired by all the exercise and excitement.

"Needs must when the devil drives," replied Meesh. Annie said nothing, but a cloud of dust billowed up from the hearth as she worked off her ill-temper with the shovel and brush.

"Were you ever in Siberia?" asked Meesh as they walked down the road together.

"No," said Willie. "And neither were you!"

"That's a matter of opinion," said Meesh.

"It's not. It's a matter of fact," said Willie.

"A fact concerning which your opinion and my opinion may differ," said Meesh.

"But still a matter of fact," persisted Willie.

"That's as it may be," said Meesh non-committally. "Anyway there's a place in Siberia called Yakutsk. It's that cold, the whisky freezes in the bottles. Man it's not safe to kiss out of doors in the winter in case your noses freeze together."

"No doubt," said Willie, scornfuly.

"I believe he's doubting my word," said Meesh to a passing seagull. "Man, I've seen couples myself going about for a whole winter yoked by their noses, until the thaw came in the spring and set them free again."

"Could they not have gone indoors and had an artificial thaw?" asked Willie.

"Not in Yakutsk," said Meesh. "You see, kissing is taboo — that's the punishment."

Willie said nothing, and they walked on in silence for a few moments. Then Meesh added slyly, "It's taboo in Crobuie as well."

"A lot of things are taboo in Crobuie," said Willie with feeling. "It's a sad thought that, in another ten years, I'll have to go elsewhere for my holidays. Crobuie will be covered with heather as if it had never existed."

"Maybe," said Meesh. Then after another silence he added. "There's some in Crobuie that defy the ban."

Willie knew the reference was to his own flirtation with the District Nurse, but he tried to hide his annoyance.

"What's all this about Yakutsk?" he asked.

"Nothing at all," said Meesh. "Except that there's colder places. Do you know, Annie stuck her fist in the fire today, right up to the elbow, and the fire went out. All she got was a wee singe on the point of the thumb."

"She did it deliberately?" asked Willie in surprise.

"Now just a minute," said Meesh. "That's an awkward question. Do you mean slowly, or intentionally?"

"Intentionally," said Willie.

"Well, she did it deliberately. As deliberately as she ever did anything in her life," said Meesh. Then he added, "You see, she knows we sent the advertisement to the paper."

"We didn't," said Willie, hotly. "You did."

"Whoever did it," said Meesh raising his voice, "It's caused a lot of trouble in this village. Innocent people suspected. Houses divided. Nothing but bad feeling and quarrelling. Stealing sheep. Attacking gamekeepers. Getting thrown in gaol. Nothing as bad as this has happened in Crobuie since I remember."

Willie looked at Meesh in amazement. Then the old salt struck his fist in the palm of his hand. "The Postmaster!" he said with conviction.

"What about him?" asked the puzzled Willie.

"Think of the opportunities he has," said Meesh, and before Willie could reply, he put his arm around his shoulder and began to whisper to him confidentially.

"You know," he said, "the way you can sense when there's a rat in the barn, although he's quite still, watching you from a corner and you're not seeing him at all."

"I suppose I do," said Willie. "But I dont see the point."

"It's Maggie Moogish," said Meesh. "She was behind the peat-stack gathering fuel. I didnt see her. I didn't hear her. I didn't smell her. But I know she was there."

"You want her to blame the Postmaster?" asked Willie.

"I'm not above doing a man a good turn," said Meesh.

"It's bad enough making trouble without casting the blame on other people," said Willie.

"Trouble," said Meesh. "Man, if they think he's on the look-out for someone they'll be in his shop all day buying things they don't need. If only I had a share in his businesss."

They walked on a few hundred yards, then Meesh turned for home. "It's time to put about ship," he said.

"What is it now?" asked Willie.

"Maggie has a fair start," said Meesh. "She's had time to pick up Bellag on the way. The convoy will be at anchor by the time we reach."

"You mean Maggie will be calling on Annie?" asked Willie.

"Precisely," said Meesh, "and if we slip in quietly and hide in the porch, we can hear what they're saying."

By the time they had reached their listening post, just as Meesh had foreseen, Maggie and Bellag had got over the preliminaries and had come to the main topic.

"I know who it is," said Maggie decisively.

"Who?" asked the others in chorus.

"Who but the Postmaster," said Maggie in a "don't dare contradict me" tone of voice.

"The dainty Davy," said Bellag with scorn.

"Surely not," said Annie, not quite ready to jump to unwarranted conclusions.

"He's the very man," said Maggie belligerently. "Fine I know it."

"How can you know it?" asked Annie incredulously.

"I know," said Maggie, and that was that.

"There's no need for the Postmaster to get married. He has a sister there and she worships the ground he walks on. He won't get a wife to do that," said Annie.

"Many a man has thrown his sister overboard before now," said Maggie. "They're all selfish dogs when it comes to that."

"Besides, he's the only one in the village that would go to the newspapers for a wife," added Maggie. "He's that stuck up, he won't open the shop in the morning until he has a collar on. I saw him myself putting on a bowler hat to go down the croft with the hen's brochan. The wind blew his hat off — and serve him right."

Annie was annoyed at the disrespectful tone which Maggie used towards the Postmaster but relieved at the indication that there was nothing between them.

"Who but the Postmaster could put a notice in the paper without the Postmaster knowing?" asked Maggie clinching her argument.

Meesh in the porch was doubled up with laughter. "Maggie should have been a lawyer," he whispered to Willie.

"I think she's right, Annie," said Bellag.

"The Postmaster doesn't open the letters," said Annie heatedly.

"How do you know?" asked Maggie.

"I don't know — but he's not that sort of man," said Annie.

"Who else in Crobuie would want to marry a lady?" asked Maggie.

"That's what the paper said," agreed Bellag, who always sided with the ship carrying the heavier guns. "With a view to matrimony."

"Who but the Postmaster would want a matrimony?" asked Maggie triumphantly. "Weddings are good enough for the likes of us."

"He'll buy her fur-lined boots at the first go-off," said Bellag, a little wistfully.

"If he gets anyone," said Maggie with venom.

"There'll be no living in the village with her. An English accent, and a permanent wave, and fur boots going to the well." Bellag seemed to have a fixation where fur boots were concerned.

"The Postmaster will have to clean the byre himself after this," said Maggie more pointedly. "It's myself that will laugh when I see her going down the croft picking her steps like a hen with the chilblains. If she ever goes down it at all!"

Maggie by now knew not only that the advertisement was inserted by the Postmaster, she had a perfect picture in her mind of the sort of wife he would get!

Meesh and Willie almost gave themselves away trying to see her give a flat-footed imitation of a dainty, town-bred woman coping with the mud on a Lewis croft after a rainy winter.

"A little doll with a painted face, the size of an eireag's* egg," she concluded.

"And plucked eyebrows, too, like the magazine we got from Detroit," agreed Bellag.

Then Maggie took another tack. She thought she had a real grievance this time against the imaginary bride. "Do you think she'll give a hand loading a lorry of peats? No fear. We'll have to do her share and our own as well. She'll treat us like a crowd of scallags.** I know fine what she'll be like — a lump of sugar candy, with a hat on the side of her head, like a jelly that didn't set. I'll never go into the Post Office again."

"Neither will I," echoed Bellag, "supposing I never get another packet of Rinso as long as I live."

"I don't believe the Postmaster had anything to do with it, and it's not fair to be blaming him," said Annie emphatically.

"If he didn't do it, who did?" asked Maggie thrusting her face into Annie's as if she was going to snap at her very tonsils.

"I don't know," said Annie quietly, "But I'm going to find out." She said it with such quiet assurance that even Maggie was impressed.

"How will you do that?" asked Bellag curiously.

"Very easily," said Annie.

Behind the door of the porch Meesh looked a little less cocky than he had been. Annie was a force to reckon with in her quiet mood.

"Just listen to this," said Annie. "We've all written replies to that advertisement."

"Speak for yourself," said Maggie.

"There's no good trying to hide it," said Annie. "We all wrote, but Katag is the only one who had a chance to post."

"That's quite true," agreed Bellag. Maggie stubbornly said nothing.

Annie unfolded her plan. They would all post their replies on different days. The newspaper would forward them to the advertiser, and, if he lived in Crobuie, the unusual stream of correspondence would unmask him.

"You're for the high jump," whispered Willie to Meesh behind the door, and he meant it, but Meesh just grinned.

"There's not a house in the village but there's a woman in it. If we all stick together we're bound to find out," said Annie emphatically.

"When we do, I'll make marags of him," said Maggie viciously, thinking of the long puddings of meal and blood and suet she used to make in the intestines of a sheep, when it was lawful to kill one and salt it down for the winter.

"I was the first to write my letter," said Bellag, staking a claim. She said no more, but Maggie read her like a book. If the advertiser were not from Crobuie after all, the first reply might walk away with the prize before the others had a chance. Always assuming that he was not already engaged to Katag — a horrible fear that haunted every woman in the village.

---

* a young hen   ** the lowest form of servant

"You were the first to write. I'll be the first to post," said Maggie, her jaw thrust out aggressively.

Meesh gave Willie a great blow in the ribs with his elbow. "Who's for the high jump now," he whispered.

"We'll draw lots," said Annie, the practical. "We're not going to quarrel now when we have the old devil on the run — whoever he is!"

Both Meesh and Willie felt that she had raised her voice in challenge when she spoke. They sensed that she not only guessed their part in the plot, but also knew that they were eavesdropping.

Annie's plan was accepted, and the three women hurried out through the kitchen to round up the rest of the village and make their plans. Habukkuk was telling Peigi for the tenth time about the "c-c-court" and Meesh's triumph, when Bellag popped her head round the door, and without a word summoned Peigi out.

"Man," said Habakkuk to Willie later in the evening, "there's something c-c-crooked g-g-going on in this village." His drooping horseshoe moustache twitched and danced with unusual animation when he described the silent signal from Bellag, Peigi's sudden disappearance and the smile of satisfaction on her face when she came back.

"I w-w-wonder what B-B-Bellag was after?" he mused, but Willie said nothing. He knew the worst, but it seemed relatively unimportant now. For the first time in their acquaintance, he and Meesh had quarrelled seriously.

Chapter XXII

The quarrel arose soon after Annie, Bellag and Maggie Moogish had dashed off to lay their trap. As soon as they were safely on their way Meesh and Willie left their uncomfortable observation post and settled at the kitchen fire to discuss the situation.

"You'll have to marry one of them now," said Willie affably. "What about Maggie Moogish?"

"Not on your life!" said Meesh with feeling. "Her jaw goes snap, snap, snap all day like an alligator."

"I've never seen an alligator," said Willie, "You see I'm an educated man!"

He smiled at his own sharpness in anticipating Meesh's inevitable remark.

"All the same, you're learning," said Meesh smiling proudly at his pupil.

"It's all right, joking," said Willie, "But I think Annie knows."

"I wouldn't be surprised," said Meesh. "She can hear a cat purring through three closed doors when you don't want her to. It's an awful calamity that men can't talk in private without women eavesdropping."

Willie reminded him that he had just been eavesdropping himself. That was entirely different, countered Meesh. Women did their eavesdropping out of sheer, ungovernable curiosity, but he had a sublime constructive purpose behind his. "How can I carry out my plan," he asked, "if I don't know what they're saying?"

"Plan!" laughed Willie, mirthlessly. "If the women intercept these letters they'll have a plan — they'll make mincemeat of you."

"I wouldn't worry at all."

"You'll have to worry!" said Willie.

"I don't know what they do to a man's brains when they educate him," said Meesh sadly. Then he began to explain his next move as if talking to a little child. "We're sending a wire to the paper telling them not to post the replies. The first day you're in town you'll collect them. We'll have the time of our lives reading all the proposals. We better do it now while we still have time."

Willie looked at the darkening sky. The sun was gone. Black clouds were heaping up from the south west. There was a smell of rain in the air. Crogorm — the nearest telegraph office — was a good five miles each way across the moor, and by nightfall it would be sheeting down.

"We've got to pay for our fun, my lad. That's one of the rules of life," said Meesh interpreting Willie's thought from the apprehensive look he gave the sky.

"I'll go with you," said Willie reluctantly, but just then a knock at the door introduced a new situation and sparked their quarrel off.

Knocking was unusual in Crobuie. People walked in and out of each other's houses unannounced. Willie looked at Meesh in surprise. "Will I answer the door?" asked Willie when he saw that Meesh made no move to go.

"It's no one of any importance," said Meesh. "A tinker, or an Indian pedlar with a pack on his back — or maybe an official from the Department of Agriculture. No one from the village would knock."

Willie thought they had seen enough of officials for one summer holiday, but, before he could frame a suitable comment Annie came bustling in from the scullery. Willie was obviously surprised to see her back so soon. He wondered when she had come and how much more she had heard. Meesh was equally surprised, but he gave no visible sign.

"Two grown men, and you haven't the gumption to open the door for the Postmaster," said Annie as she passed through on her way to the front door.

"He would knock," said Meesh in a tone which implied that all who did so belonged to an inferior race beyond the pale.

"I'm sorry the fire is in the kitchen, but we weren't expecting visitors," said Annie ushering the Postmaster in, and indicating a seat by the fire.

"I can't sit," he protested pompously. "I'm a busy man," he didn't quite crow, but he tended to strut self-consciously, like a hen that has just laid an egg.

"If half the men in this village worked as hard as you, the women would have an easier time," said Annie pointedly.

"We can't all make a living selling penny stamps," said Meesh good naturedly.

"You couldn't make a living in a gold-mine — you're too lazy to fill your pockets," snapped Annie.

The Postmaster was impatient, although he tried to hide it.

"I would like to speak to your brother — privately," he said as politely as possible, but he knew it was rather an affront to a Crobuie woman to ask her to withdraw from what promised to be an interesting conversation.

"I hope you don't think I can't hold my tongue," said Annie. "I can be as tight as a clam, but if you have any secrets, don't trust that chatterbox. He has less sense than a gramophone."

The Postmaster was covered in confusion. He didn't want to offend Annie. That was obvious. But he wanted desperately to have a private talk with Meesh.

"I have every confidence in your complete discretion, but this is a matter strictly between men," he replied in his prim, pompous way.

"That's all right," said Annie laughing. "Anyway I have a cow to milk."

"Thank the Lord there's a cow to milk now and then," said Meesh after the departing Annie, but she didn't pause to make the obvious reply. She wanted the Postmaster to see that she could be discreet.

"Is she always in a bad temper?" asked the Postmaster in a confidential whisper as Annie left them. He seemed quite put out.

"Annie has a heart of gold," laughed Meesh, and he meant it.

Then he added with a smile, "she's a wee bit crusty these days — like every other spinster in Crobuie."

The Postmaster nodded his head wisely.

"I don't know what's got into them," he said. "Since we came back from gaol, I haven't had a moment's peace in my place of business."

"Hero-worship," said Meesh. "They've heard how you diddled the Sheriff." He winked at Willie, but the Postmaster missing the irony swelled like a pouter pigeon. He fully believed it was he who got them out of trouble. He had told Katag as much, and he was glad to hear Meesh confirm it.

"He can't even call a shop a shop," said Meesh to himself, but not even Willie caught the flicker of disgust which crossed his face.

Willie, in fact, was too busy wondering why the Postmaster was being pestered by the women. It had obviously been Meesh's intention that he should be, but that little ploy was now short-circuited by Annie's stratagem.

"One at a time is good fishing, but it's better when you get two with one hook," said Meesh irrelevantly. The Postmaster looked at him, with a puzzled frown, but Willie knew it was the answer to this own unspoken question. There must have been more than Maggie within earshot at the peat-stack.

"I can't sell a pound of margarine today, without getting dog's abuse," said the Postmaster quite oblivious of the unspoken conversation going on around him. "If I wasn't a servant of the Crown I would slam the door in their faces. I would let them whistle for their tea, and their matches, and their paraffin."

"Why then did you advertise?" asked Meesh. The question came like the crack of a whip, and the Postmaster jumped from his chair with surprise and vexation.

"I had no hand in it whatsoever," he shouted.

"Who else could it be?"

"That is precisely what I intend to find out," said the Postmaster drawing himself up to the full extent of his five foot four. "And that's precisely why I have come to you."

"You don't think I'm mad enough to put a notice like that in the paper," asked Meesh innocently.

"On the contrary, I would never dream of suspecting you," said the Postmaster. " 'If there's one person in Crobuie who'll never be married, it's Meesh,' that's what I said to myself, and that's why I'm here."

"I would like fine to catch the devil that did it, but I don't see how we can," said Meesh, with a broad grin at Willie behind the Postmaster's back.

"Oh yes, we'll catch him," said the Postmaster, rubbing his hands. "This is very subtle. I'm not a commercial genius for nothing. There's no use asking who did it, because the culprit won't tell. He won't get married now, even if he gets an answer — he'll be too scared. But, if we try to find out all those who didn't do it, then obviously the one man in the village who didn't not do it, is the man who did."

"Sounds like a conundrum to me," said Meesh.

"It's quite simple if you have a head for business," said the Postmaster.

"I have a paper here," he continued, handing the sheet to Meesh. "The Missionary was in the Post Office today and I asked his advice. I drafted it myself of course, but I consulted him. Two heads are better than one."

"Even when one is the Postmaster's," said Meesh.

The Postmaster let the jibe go by.

"It's not a proclamation of marriage is it?" asked Willie innocently.

"No," said the Postmaster sharply. "It's a very solemn declaration, in these terms — 'I, the undersigned, being resident in Crobuie, an adult male of sound mind and a bachelor, do solemnly swear, on soul and conscience, that I am not responsible for the matrimonial advertisement appearing in the current issue of the 'St Kilda Sun'. ''

"Do you think the women of Crobuie will believe you — even if you shout it from the housetops," said Meesh with a gesture of disgust. "Some of these gossiping old cailleachs can read your thoughts before you think them."

"That's the point," said the Postmaster briskly. "I'm taking this to every bachelor in Crobuie to sign. The one that won't sign is the guilty party. I'm sure there's no one in the whole of Crobuie will put his name to a lie with the fiery furnace gaping at his feet."

Willie looked quizzically at Meesh to see how he was taking it, but Meesh was puffing contentedly at his pipe.

"I'll put my name down first, and then hand the paper to you," said the Postmaster.

He wrote his name with a flourish, then handed the fountain pen to Meesh.

"Take in a reef or two, my friend," said Meesh, waving the pen aside. "You're sailing too fast for an old hand like me."

"You won't sign?" asked the Postmaster, surprised.

"I didn't say that," replied Meesh cautiously.

Willie was delighted. Here was a complication Meesh had not foreseen.

"Well, here's the pen," persisted the Postmaster. "I think you should raise your right hand, the way they do in court, to make it more solemn."

"Come on, Meesh," said Willie, with a glint of devilment in his eye. "You know what they'll say if you don't sign."

"If you refuse to sign . . ." said the Postmaster significantly.

"Meesh advertising for a wife. He'll get it when Annie finds out," said Willie, unable to resist the temptation to exploit the situation.

He regretted it at once, however, because Meesh was in a real dilemma.

Willie could not imagine him getting out of it by telling a cold-blooded lie, and there seemed no other way.

"Your hesitation does you no credit," said the Postmaster.

Still Meesh made no move.

"Clouds of suspicion are gathering round your head," he added pompously.

"When I came in, I would have sworn that Meesh was innocent, but now he must prove it. I'm not taking the blame for this, one moment longer." There was a long silence.

"Give me the paper," said Meesh suddenly, as if he had reached the end of a struggle with himself.

"That's better," said the Postmaster. "I would hate to think you were the skunk."

He proffered the fountain pen to Meesh, but Meesh waved it aside. He read the paper through carefully, and then he solemnly tore it in shreds and stuffed it into the heart of the fire.

"Your bit of paper is worthless," Meesh told him before he could utter a protest. "I'm surprised that a man with so much intelligence should have so little sense. If a man is low enough to advertise for a wife, he's low enough to put his name to a lie."

"Indeed!" said Willie significantly, but Meesh paid no attention.

"Everyone in Crobuie will sign that bit of paper," continued Meesh. "Then the women will begin to ask, why was the Postmaster so anxious to prove it wasn't him? They'll answer their own question by saying, 'because it was him. He was only trying to cover his tracks'!"

The Postmaster looked upset.

"I know their nasty little minds," said Meesh pursuing his advantage. "That bit of paper would be your death warrant. You should be grateful I burnt it for you. It's the best turn I've done you in my life."

"I'm deeply grateful," said the Postmaster, looking shaken, as if he had just escaped from a wrecked ship, or an angry bull. "I'm glad I came here first."

Then another thought struck him. He had compromised himself deeply.

"Promise not to tell," he pled.

"I'll not breathe a word. Neither will he," said Meesh, indicating Willie.

"Thank you," said the Postmaster. "That's a relief."

"Of course, you can't stop folk from guessing," said Meesh, now in full pursuit. "Half the village saw you coming here today — for the first time in your life. Annie saw you with a paper in your hand. They'll be jumping to conclusions, quicker than a kitten chasing a fly."

"What can I do?" asked the Postmaster thoroughly terrified.

"Marry!" barked Meesh.

The Postmaster stepped back as if a gun had been pointed at him.

"Marry!" repeated Meesh. "Marry as quick as you can."

"Why should I, if I don't want to?" asked the Postmaster feebly.

"It's the only way you can live this scandal down," said Meesh. "The women blame you already. I heard them at it today. Coming here stupidly with a paper in your hand — that's the last straw.

"It's not your reputation — it's your business," he continued, striking at the Postmaster's tenderest spot. "Do you think the women in the village will buy tapioca from a man who insulted them?"

"But I didn't. I swear I didn't," said the terrified Postmaster.

"It doesn't matter what you did," said Meesh towering above him like threatening doom. "All that matters is what they think you did. Remember — you may be the only shop-keeper in Crobuie now, but anyone can start. A smaller thing than this has ruined a man before now."

"Go easy, Meesh," said Willie catching the old sailor by the jacket tail. "You'll scare him out of his wits."

"I'm advising him for his own good," said Meesh, as solemnly as if he really meant it.

"How will it help me, getting married?" asked the Postmaster.

"If a man can get married by asking a woman, do you think he would advertise?" said Meesh patiently as if he were explaining a simple proposition in Euclid to a first year pupil.

"Once you're safely spliced, they'll fix on some other poor devil and take it out on him."

The Postmaster was completely over-awed. Meesh could do what he liked with him.

"Do you think anyone would take me — on short notice like this?" he asked a little bashfully.

Like a skilful angler who has hooked his fish, Meesh changed his tactics to meet the new situation.

"Surely," he replied. "Think of your bank book. Think of your official position. Think of your dignified bearing. Your handsome figure. You can have the pick of Crobuie, if only you have the courage."

"I'll think it over," said the Postmaster preparing to go.

"Don't think — act," said Meesh. Then with a sly look at Willie, he added. "Go for the youngest and prettiest."

The Postmaster paused at the door. He was in a daze, like a man wakening up from a bad dream.

"Ask the District Nurse, she's a smart lass," encouraged Meesh.

"Come off it," growled Willie.

"She's a bit young for an elderly man like you, but just ask her and see what happens," said Meesh.

"Thank you," said the stricken Postmaster and stumbled off into the rain.

"What do you mean, stuffing the Postmaster with that nonsense about the District Nurse?" demanded Willie. "She wouldn't touch him with a barge pole."

"I know you have a fancy for her . ." began Meesh.

"I have nothing of the sort," interrupted Willie, hotly.

"Then what's biting you?" asked Meesh.

Willie muttered something incoherent about not interfering in other people's private affairs.

"If I don't interfere, who will?" asked Meesh, unabashed.

Then he added seriously, "Joking apart, Willie, I know you like the District Nurse, but there's nothing in it. You come for your holidays, then you're off again to the city. It's different with her. She's here for the rest of her natural life, sinking slowly in the bog. There hasn't been a marriage in this village for a dozen years. They've forgotten how to marry. There's nothing here but slow decay and desolation. It'll take an earthquake to get that girl married — that's why I've started one."

"Indeed?" said Willie sarcastically.

"She's too good for the Postmaster, I know," said Meesh interpreting Willie's thought, "but he's the only decent match in Crobuie, even if he is a self-important cockatoo."

Meesh put on his coat. "Come on Willie, it's a long way to Crogorm. We must get that telegram off."

This time he had gone too far.

"I'm not going to Crogorm," said Willie sulkily. "You dug the hole and you can darn well climb out of it yourself."

"It's a long road for an old man, alone on a stormy night," said Meesh, wheedling.

"That's your problem," said Willie sharply. "I'll see you as far as the cross roads, but after that you can shift for yourself."

They had scarcely opened the door to go when Annie pounced. She always knew when Meesh was going out.

"Where do you two think you are going on a night like this?" she asked.

"Poaching," said Meesh cheerily.

"You've chosen a grand night for it," said Annie. "It's coming down in buckets now."

"That's the idea," said Meesh composedly. "We won't be any wetter, even if we fall in the river."

Annie knew that he was hedging, and he knew that she knew. "Come on, Willie," he said hurriedly, to avoid further questions.

"Just a minute!" said Annie. "What was the Postmaster after?"

"Nothing!" said Meesh. "He just wanted advice about a paper he was signing."

"And he came to you!" said Annie sarcastically. "I don't believe it. There's not a man in the village would ask your advice about a dog licence, even if he was flaming drunk."

"He wanted my advice about the paper he had. Isn't that true Willie?" appealed Meesh.

"Yes," growled Willie, still in the sulks.

"Well, if you won't tell me, I'll just have to find out," said Annie.

"How?" asked Meesh curiously.

"I want some paraffin, and I'm going to get it. If the Postmaster chooses to tell me, it's no business of yours."

"You got paraffin today already," said Meesh.

"There's no law against getting it twice," retorted Annie.

Meesh shrugged his shoulders and went out into the rain followed by Willie.

Annie got ready to go out too. She took unusual pains smoothing her hair, and brushing her coat.

She wrote a note, read it with satisfaction and stuck it on the mantlepiece.

These preliminaries completed she followed Meesh and Willie into the rain. She had no paraffin tin and many strange things were to happen before the three of them met again a few hours later.

Chapter XXIII

Willie left Meesh at the cross-roads. "It's your funeral!" was his final salute. It was the first time in all the years of their friendship that they had parted for the night on a bitter word.

"Cheerio," said Meesh flatly, but with just that hint of warmth in the voice that might have been an overture of peace, if Willie were in the mood to take it. Willie said nothing.

Meesh looked at the rough hill path where the water was already beginning to run in rivulets. He looked into the south at the lowering sky. He looked back towards the house he had left, thinking wistfully of the warm peat fire, but all he saw was Annie muffled up, head into the wind, hurrying towards the Post Office.

"This is Cape Horn," muttered the old salt to himself. "Others got round it, why shouldn't I." He took a firm grasp of his staff and set his steps doggedly up the hill.

When he breasted the top of the rise the wind struck him like a wet cloth. The gale was so violent, he had a struggle to get his breath, and the rain came at him from all sides. Moorland puddles, scooped up by the wind, spat against his legs. Underneath his feet the ground turned into a brown and slimy porridge. His gumboots slithered and squelched as he walked. Sometimes the bog sucked at his boots as if it was trying to claw them from his feet, but he plodded on regardless.

Annie had a much shorter journey than her brother but she was wet by the time she reached the Post Office. Little diamonds of rain trickled down her nose in the light of the Tilley lamp. There was a drip, drip, drip, from her sodden coat as she stood at the counter.

"A fine night this to be going for messages," said Katag morosely.

It was a very unfriendly welcome for a good customer, thought Annie. She should be glad that anyone ventured out.

"Where's himself?" she asked, as non-committally as she could, but Katag knew at once that she hadn't come for paraffin, or barley meal, but on some private businesss with the Postmaster. Pointedly she ignored the question.

"Is he out?" asked Annie hesitantly. It was a delicate matter repeating a question of that sort.

"It looks like it," said Katag. "He's not under the counter anyway."

"I see that," said Annie, flatly, not quite sure of the next move.

"You can't see it," said Katag, determined to be hostile. "You didn't look?"

Annie obligingly looked over the counter, as if to make sure the

Postmaster was not below it. Neither of them saw the funny side of the situation. Each was too taut with her own particular problem.

"You got your messages already today," said Katag, after a pause.

"Most of them," said Annie, picking a carton off the counter and reading, or appearing to read, the recipe for macaroni au gratin.

"That's just sgudal," said Katag, using an expressive Gaelic word for which English has no equivalent. "I wouldn't feed it to the hens."

Normally Katag was a keen and efficient saleswoman and Annie would have been puzzled and worried by the reception she got, were it not that she was even more puzzled and worried by the Postmaster's absence.

"Will he be long?" she asked at length.

It required a good deal of courage for a woman in Crobuie to ask so direct a question concerning the movements of a man. In the dying village everyone used subterfuge to depolarise the reactions between the sexes. The men and women were on friendly enough terms most of the time, but, while the women were women among themselves, and the men, men, among men, when the two sexes mingled, or spoke of each other, an odd, impersonal, allusive mode of speech was resorted to, instinctively, as a neutraliser.

"Long?" echoed Katag. "How should I know? I'm only his sister."

She was angry with her brother, and Annie sensed that her anger arose from something that touched the taboo. Her own anxiety increased accordingly.

"Do you know were he's gone?" she asked, plunging boldly into the forbidden.

"He went to see the District Nurse," said Katag, and before the sentence was completed Annie was gone. The door slammed behind her with a crack that shattered the glass.

Katag had never been known to swear, and she didn't even then, but there was profanity in her very movements as she nailed a piece of cardboard over the hole, to keep the hurricane at bay.

A hurricane it was now, screaming through the night, with an occasional high pitched rasping as if great sheets of cloth were being torn asunder over-head. But the storm without was nothing to the storm within. Though none of them realised it, just at that moment, Crobuie's long sleep was over: the whole village was in an agony of birth, as hot blood pumped once more through hardened arteries, and the dead came painfully to life.

The Postmaster was the first to feel the pangs. When he left Meesh, he closeted himself for hours in his bedroom, trying to summon up courage to propose to Marion, the District Nurse.

It needed courage. He knew he was imcomparably the most important man in Crobuie. No woman in her senses would refuse him. But the District Nurse was young, light-hearted, even light-headed. It was rumoured she was having an affair with Willie, that good-for-nothing college scamp.

"She ought to accept me," the Postmaster assured himself. There was no question of that. But she might refuse him. She might laugh in his face.

She might even go blabbing about it through the village. His pride revolted at the thought. He must never expose himself to that indignity.

On the other hand, if she did accept him, how could he break the news to Katag? All her life had been spent in his service. She had nagged him, bullied him, pushed him around, but for all that she worshipped the ground he walked on, and she had maintained his dignity at all times in the eyes of the outside world. His conscience told him it would be shabby to give her the door at her time of life, but his conscience was only a ventriloquist's dummy for his deep unacknowledged terror of his sister: if he married Marion, she would surely flay him!

But while these petrifying shadows loomed across the path, there was an even greater fear urging him on: the gnawing anxiety Meesh had planted, that his reputation, his business, everything he lived for, would be lost unless he could clear himself in the sight of these gossiping harpies. Fool! Fool! Fool! Why had he gone through the village to Meesh with that paper in his hand?

Even as the storm raged and he struggled to weigh the hazards of the two courses open to him, the issue was taken out of his hands. Before he planted the seed of anxiety, Meesh had planted the seed of desire. The women reacted to the advertisement immediately. The poison, if poison it was, worked more slowly on the men, but at last like the scare-crows in Maggie's satire, they began to think of marriage, or rather, not think, but feel — an impulse unrecognised, but irresistible. After a long unnatural winter, Spring had come to Crobuie.

By this time the Postmaster's mind was made up, but there was a practical difficulty. So many years had passed since anyone made love in Crobuie, he didn't know how to begin.

In the old days when life coursed merrily along, the practice of bundling prevailed, though it was known by a Gaelic name meaning "watch of the night". A young man, decently, under cover of darkness, could go to his sweetheart's house, to do his courting, in warmth and comfort, below the blankets. The practice was hedged about by the strictest sanctions, and in spite of appearances, the Crobuie people were moral and restrained.

The prim little Postmaster saw nothing wrong in the practice of bundling — as Crobuie had practised it, there was nothing wrong — but he could not bring himself to clamber through Marion's window in the dead of night, invading not only her bedroom, but her bed. It was unthinkable, but how else could he proceed?

He knew that in the godless, abandoned cities, a man thought nothing of going brazenly to his sweetheart's door, and asking her to walk with him in the park, or go to a cinema or dance-hall. Crobuie had no cinema or dance hall, and although, in a sense, it was one vast park, it would be shockingly indecent to walk about in the open air in the company of a woman. Besides there was the weather. The rain was rattling on the windows like machine gun fire, and the slates on the Post Office roof clattered like ill-fitting teeth.

Suddenly the Postmaster remembered his flowers. He boasted the only garden in Crobuie, if garden it could be called. The winds which devastated the island not only in winter, but sometimes in the height of summer, made gardening a most unrewarding occupation. Flowers could only survive where there were weeds to shelter them, and one had to grope among the thistles for spindly tulips, and sorry-looking marigolds, in their appropriate season. But still they were flowers, and in the Postmaster's eyes they were wonderful. Perhaps they might speak to Marion on his behalf.

Donning his oilskin and his gumboots, he lit the hurricane lamp, and crept into the garden, as furtive as a burglar. The cracksman who feels a policeman's grasp on his collar just as the safe swings open, could not be more terrified than the Postmaster gathering his own flowers in utter secrecy, and expecting every moment to see Katag, his sister, materialise among the dockens.

At last he had gathered a posy of sorts. The rain was coursing down the back of his neck. The wind had blown his lantern out. He was cold, wet, miserable, and terrified of the ordeal before him. But he daren't venture into the house again. He skirted round it on tip-toe, closed the garden gate behind him with as little noise as possible, although the wind by now would have drowned an exploding bomb, and, grasping the flowers tight against his chest, he began to run.

In spite of all his precautions, Katag, with a sister's intuition, knew where he had gone and suspected why. She had even planned some counter-measures of her own.

To say that Marion was surprised to see the Postmaster is a gross understatement. Although he was chairman of the nursing committee, and might legitimately have something to say to her, he would never, in ordinary circumstances, have ventured to her house without a chaperon. Besides a man who liked his comforts would not be abroad in any circumstances on such a night. And the flowers! For a Crobuie man to walk through the village carrying flowers, even in the darkness, was a gross defiance of social custom: it was eccentric, it was mad. Most of the men would sooner have cherished a rattle-snake.

Marion politely, if wonderingly, asked him in, and persuaded him to put off his oilskin coat.

"Aren't they lovely," she said when he handed her a skimpy bunch of ill-assorted flowers, with a vague motion of the body which might have been intended as a bow.

"The people here have no appreciation of the beautiful," said the Postmaster. "Their souls never rise above turnips." He had been rehearsing his little speech all the way along through the storm, because he felt that, in proposing to someone so much younger than himself, he must establish a poetic and romantic character.

"I'll put them in a vase," said Marion, hurrying off. The Postmaster was flattered that his gift was so highly thought of, but Marion was only making time to gather her wits, and consider how to cope with the situation.

The Postmaster, she feared, was surely wrong in the head.

"There aren't many men in Crobuie would carry flowers through the village," she said when she returned, after as long a delay as she could decently contrive.

"If there were more ladies like you in Crobuie, there might be more men like me," said the Postmaster in a characteristic amalgam of gallantry and boastfulness.

Marion had nothing to say in reply. Her mind was a blank, and she dreaded the next development in this unfortunate conversation.

There was no one in the village sufficiently ill to justify an urgent visit, and even if she adopted that ruse, the Postmaster might offer to go with her down the road. Once they were outside in the darkness, anything might happen, if he was really mad. She considered offering him a cup of tea, and drugging it, to keep him quiet while she ran for help, but that was too risky, even for such a desperate situation.

"Did you want to see me on business?" she asked at last.

"I would hardly call it business," said the Postmaster ardently, "and yet, it's the most important business of my life."

"Oh," said Marion non-committally, poking the fire although it did not need it. The poker she felt was safer at her side of the hearth than his.

The Postmaster rose. Marion tensed herself. He crossed the room with a brisk, purposeful step; stopped uncertainly, waved his arms about as if they didn't belong to him, then clutched his lapels, and cleared his throat, as if he were about to address a political meeting.

"I have a good croft," he began with unction.

"Yes," assented Marion. It was a harmless enough proposition, even for a lunatic.

"The best in the village."

"I'm sure it is," said Marion. It was best to humour him, and anyway the claim was probably justified.

"It's in my own name. My sister has nothing to do with it."

Again Marion indicated assent, although she had no knowledge of the facts. At last, however, she was seeing a little daylight. The Postmaster was suffering from delusions. He thought his sister was trying to deprive him of the croft. Where land was essential to life, and had been won, only two generations before, after a bitter struggle with rapacious landlords, it was quite a common delusion, among those who were mentally unstable. It was a shock to find the Postmaster was one of them, but as a Nurse, she was used to shocks.

"It's a very responsible position," continued the Postmaster. "There's no man in Crobuie carries such a burden."

Marion might have felt that she carried an even heavier burden as the sole nurse in a stricken village, miles from a telephone, let alone a doctor, but she was genuinely sorry that the Postmaster's mind had yielded under the strain.

"But still," continued the Postmaster. "It carries dignity, position, and if I may say so, a very reasonable income."

The smugness in the Postmaster's voice made her hastily revise her estimate. He was not suffering from delusions about the croft. It was something different. Something worse. She looked up apprehensively and read it in his eye.

"Besides, there's my business," said the Postmaster, gazing soulfully down at her. "Crobuie is not what it was. We can all see that. Still, everyone must come to me. It's the only shop!"

Very confidentially he bent towards her and whispered, "I have money in the bank!" Then feeling he might have compromised himself with someone who might shortly have a say in the spending of it, he pulled himself together and added, "Well, it's more a matter for me than for my wife how much I have."

"Wife?" asked Marion, terrified.

"Surely," said the Postmaster. "You can't be such a fool as to refuse."

Fortunately for Marion's sanity, and the Postmaster's safety, before she could say or do anything desperate, a violent gust of wind filled the room, lifting the cloth from the table, swinging the pictures dementedly on the walls, and swirling ash and smoke about until one could hardly see. From the centre of the storm came Annie, like a rocket or a jet-propelled plane.

"What's wrong?" asked Marion, jumping to her feet. She was glad to see Annie, but she was a good nurse, and relief for herself was followed instantly by anxiety for someone else. There must have been a death, or a serious injury, perhaps a scalding, to account for Annie's haste. "I'll get my bag," she added, before Annie had time to reply.

"I just want to borrow a little baking powder," said Annie, as casually as she could. A glance assured her that nothing irrevocable had happened, and it was only then she realised she must have some excuse for a visit on such a night.

"Baking powder?" said Marion in amazement. "You know I never bake. I haven't the time."

Before Annie could retrieve her blunder, the Postmaster attacked her from the other side.

"You didn't come all this distance through the storm for a little baking powder!" he said in an aggrieved tone. It wasn't like Annie to pass his shop.

"I did call at the shop," said Annie, telling the truth and lying at the same time.

"I don't suppose she could find it," said the Postmaster with a shake of the head. "If she was in charge, I would be bankrupt in a month."

Annie did not agree with the Postmaster's assessment of Katag's ability, far from it, but the opportunity was too good to miss. She had recovered her poise, and was ready to control the situation as firmly as Meesh himself might do.

"It's a shame to see you behind the counter, selling pats of butter when you have more important things to do," she said.

The Postmaster glowed. He had been annoyed when Annie interrupted his tete-a-tete, but a comment like that was a salve indeed.

"I've felt for a long time," he said pompously, "that a man of my capacity is wasting his time, counting out a score of salt herring for Bellag, and a pound of tapioca for Maggie Moogish, and all the work of the Post Office to do."

The work of the Post Office could be done in half an hour a week, as Annie knew well, and there was little hope of any expansion in Crobuie, but she knew the line of talk the Postmaster liked.

"It could be a good business," she said, "if only you had someone to leave behind the counter while you attended to the books and the correspondence."

"Yes, indeed," said the Postmaster. "But where can a man of business find servants today?"

"You would be good in a shop," said Marion, to Annie.

It had taken her a few moments to size the situation up, it was so unexpected in Crobuie to fine oneself part of an emotional triangle, but, now that she knew where she stood, she was determined to solve the problem in the way most satisfactory for everyone, especially herself.

"You think so?" asked Annie coyly.

"I'm sure of it," said Marion warmly, and she meant it. She had a high opinion of Annie's ability, as indeed she might. "You're a very capable woman. I can do poultices and bandages, and all that sort of thing, but I can't add two and two to save my life."

"Two and two is very important in a shop," said the Postmaster sagely, retiring into his thoughts, as if he were taking an important legal question to avizandum.

"I would like fine to have a shop of my own," said Annie, and the Postmaster, startled, returned from avizandum with a frown.

"Once or twice I thought of starting one," she added with a sly look at the Postmaster to see how he was taking it, and Marion thought how like the gesture was to Meesh.

"Why didn't you start?" asked Marion.

"We haven't a room to spare," said Annie, as if that were a calamity. By now the Postmaster was thoroughly upset. There were plenty of rooms in the village, if Annie had a mind to start, and she was so popular she would have no difficulty in getting one.

"It's a serious step, opening a shop when you have no previous experience," said the Postmaster, feeling that he was very cunningly sowing doubt. "It's easier to lose money than to make it."

He paused for a moment to let the words sink in, and then he asked, "Do you really think there's custom enough in Crobuie to start another shop?"

"Annie would soon make custom," said Marion with conviction, and the Postmaster was afraid that it was true.

"It's only a notion," said Annie with a deprecating gesture. "Nothing may come of it."

Put that way, the advent of competition seemed really imminent.

"If you'll just step over to the shop with me, I'll get you the baking powder," said the Postmaster hurriedly.

Marion pressed them both to stay for a cup of tea. It was the Crobuie custom to be open-handed, but, quite apart from that, she was now begnning to enjoy the situation, and had visions of a pleasant night in store. But Annie and the Postmaster were both determined to go. Annie had pressing reasons of her own, quite unconnected with baking powder, while the Postmaster, for his part, was anxious to get out of his compromising situation with Marion. He saw now the folly that Meesh had led him into with his nonsense about the District Nurse: it was obviously a ruse to head him off from Annie, who was far and away the matrimonial prize of the village. "Five more minutes and I might have been married to the wrong one," he told himself, under his breath.

As they rose to go, Marion offered them a torch — the Postmaster's lantern was quite unserviceable in the gale, which was howling like the day of judgment.

"Never mind the torch," said the Postmaster brushing it aside.

"We'll be all right in the dark," said Annie, with lightness and music in her voice such as Crobuie had not heard for a generation.

The door had scarcely closed behind them when Marion was startled once again by an urgent knocking. She opened it cautiously, and found Willie there, wetter than the night he fell in the river.

It was dead against the conventions of Crobuie for him to call. It was a more serious lapse even than the Postmaster's. After all, the Postmaster was an oldish man, and might have had business to discuss about the Nursing Committee, but Willie was an acknowledged lover, carried there by the tide of his feelings, and by that alone. If Marion had been living with her parents no one would have thought it odd to see Willie tip-toe to her room at dead of night, but she lived alone, and he came in the early evening when lights were on. That was occasion for a scandal, indeed.

Marion gave no thought to convention when she saw him there. The fire that Meesh had started was fanning through Crobuie. Marion was reckless, happy and alive.

"I'll make you a cup of tea while you're drying off," said Marion, when she had ushered Willie in and he was standing steaming in front of a roaring fire.

"What a night it's been," she added, pausing at the door, with a smile of mingled certainty and doubt. Bright, magical, mysterious, like moonrise in a clear sky.

"A night indeed," agreed Willie, still wondering how he ever plucked up courage to come.

Outside, in the storm, Annie and the Postmaster were shyly but happily groping their way together through the dark.

Meesh was groping too, as he struggled home from Crogorm. The wind and the rain, and the state of the moor, had delayed him so much that he arrived too late to send his wire. Disconsolately he trudged homeward to a situation more desperate than he knew.

Chapter XXIV

The Missionary was furious when Bellag thrust him into the storm to go to the Post Office for food.

"If the cat ate the pudding it was your own fault," he growled.

"If the cat ate the pudding it's you that'll be hungry," responded Bellag. The Missionary had quite a healthy appetite, and he took the hint, muffling his coat around his throat to keep the rain at bay.

"Another fool on the ran-dan," was Katag's salute, as he entered, stumbling on the threshold in his hurry to get out of the rain.

"Who's on the ran-dan?" he asked sharply. As Missionary it was his duty, as well as his pleasure, to be informed of any little titbit of gossip. Not that Crobuie normally provided much.

"I was fair scandalised," said Katag. "You never saw anything like it in your life."

"What was it?" asked the Missionary, moved by a curious mixture of hope and fear that it might be something really dreadful. Something he might get a sermon out of.

"My brother," said Katag, viciously. "There's not much sense there, even if he is my own flesh and blood."

"I have the greatest respect for the Postmaster," said the Missionary, perturbed by this turn of events. A scandal concerning the Postmaster would rock Crobuie to the foundations. It would be almost as bad as if he got involved himself, and he was incorruptible.

"It's that woman," said Katag, adding to the Missionary's curiosity, and telling him nothing.

"Woman?" he asked in horror, stepping back from the chasm that seemed to have opened at his feet, right in the middle of the Post Office floor.

"I just happened to say that he was seeing the District Nurse, about business, and there she was, out the door like a dog chasing a rat."

The Missionary, still bewildered, but gradually realising that the situation was indeed grave, looked solemnly at the door as if the mysterious "she" would dart out again in pursuit of the Postmaster just to illustrate Katag's narrative.

"Half an hour later," said Katag, with great dramatic emphasis. "Half an our later they came back — arm in arm."

"Arm in arm?" said the Missionary aghast. He could not have been more thoroughly shocked if he had caught the Postmaster stealing from the collection plate on Communion Sunday.

"Arm in arm," said Katag. "There's no decency or modesty left at all."

"I'll have to call the kirk session," said the Missionary. "Even though he is your brother."

"I don't mind for that," said Katag. "But what can the kirk session do?"

"Discipline," said the Missionary solemnly. "They have the power."

"That won't help if they're all in the same boat," said Katag.

"You think there are others?" asked the Missionary in dismay.

The Church did not frown on marriage as such, but it frowned on innovation, and in Crobuie it was almost an innovation to walk down the street, so lifeless had the village become, let alone go arm in arm through the dark.

"What one can do, another can do," said Katag, and although the Missionary did not notice it, there was almost a hint of invitation in her voice.

The Missionary was anxious to get home as quickly as possible now. He was afraid some reckless philanderer might have spirited Bellag away in the few moments since he left. A man must be on his guard these days. The devil was stalking abroad.

"Arm in arm!" he muttered, as he turned to go, quite forgetful of the errand on which he had come.

"Arm in arm," echoed Katag, and this time the invitation was so unmistakable even the Missionary felt the siren call. He made to go, but felt rooted to the spot.

"I can hardly believe it," he said with a sigh as if all the sins of the universe rested on his back. "Arm in arm," he added, and Katag, alert to every nuance, detected in the tone a faint response to her own advances.

"I'll show you," she said, and before the Missionary could move she was advancing towards him round the end of the counter.

"Tut, tut, tut," he spluttered in agitation. "That would never do."

With a swiftness of movement of which Katag hardly believed him possible, he slammed the door shut against any prying eyes, and slipped home the bolt.

"Now you can show me," he said.

It was just at that moment Bellag arrived to see what had happened to her brother. Exercising a neighbour's privilege she came through the Postmaster's house to save a few yards of walking in the rain, and caught the guilty pair, in flagrante delicto.

The Missionary dropped Katag's arm as if it were red hot, but Katag gripped him again, as tight as a vice. Facing up to Bellag, boldly she announced, "We've just got engaged."

"So have I," said Bellag calmly.

"Then I'll have to take her, right enough," said the Missionary, linking Katag's arm again. It was no compliment to Katag, but she showed little resentment. She was too happy nestling his arm against her side.

"When did this happen?" asked Katag, not that she cared very much, her own engagement was pleasure enough for an evening without worrying about anyone else's.

"It's been in the air for a long time," replied Bellag, although they all knew that was a lie. "But it came to a head sudden like, just after himself left the house." She nodded towards her brother.

"Man," said the Missionary in a voice of awe, "It can strike you down in a minute, like the fork lightning."

"Who is it?" asked Katag at last. She hoped that Bellag would volunteer the information and render a question unnecessary. It detracted from her own proper omniscience that she had to ask a detail of that sort about anyone in Crobuie.

"A dear friend," said Bellag, with tantalising vagueness. "A very old friend indeed."

Katag was baffled. They were all old friends in the village for that matter, and she had never seen Bellag show any partiality for one man more than another, or any man at all show partiality for her.

The Missionary began to guess. The only system he could think of was to take the village croft by croft and name the men in turn. Bellag had dismissed more than nine tenths of Crobuie with a haughty "No," before the Missionary said "Habakkuk," but when he did she blushed like the blacksmith's forge in the days when horses were still shod and maidens still married in the village.

"Where is he?" asked Katag, surprised that anyone in Crobuie, having just acquired a man, should be so careless as to let him out of her sight.

"That's the funny thing," said Bellag. "He popped into the house as soon as himself was gone, and asked me to marry him. It took a long time with the stutter before I was sure that's what he meant, and as soon as I said yes, he asked for the murtair."

Murtair is the Gaelic word for murderer, but the term is most generally applied to a lethal apparatus for poaching salmon, consisting of three or four large iron fish hooks tied together back to back so that the barbs stick out like the flukes of an anchor.

"The Murtair?" said the Missionary perplexed. "That's an odd thing for a man to want at a reiteach."

A reiteach is a pre-marriage celebration: a sort of engagement party. In the days of old it had often rivalled the wedding itself as a festivity. The Missionary wondered whether there was some old custom associated with the reiteach that he had forgotten. He racked his brains for an answer, because he would hate to let Katag down by neglecting any of the traditions, now that he was reconciled, more or less, to the prospect of marrying her, but he could see no possible use for a murtair.

"He said something about the well," said Bellag, after a pause. "I couldn't understand him. Our well is the best in the village, but he said it was the well at the bottom of his own croft."

"He won't catch much in any well, murtair or no murtair," said Katag significantly.

"What's more, the well at the bottom of his croft is bone dry," said the Missionary. "There hasn't been a drop of water in it since the year Winter's brown cow dropped twins, and that was in the year of the Crimea." The Missionary's chronology was a little bit askew but Winter and the Crimea went hand in hand.

"Do you think? asked Katag, cryptically, touching her temple. The Missionary said nothing, but gently disengaged her arm. if Habakkuk was out of his mind, then Bellag would not be getting married, and there would be no need for him to get married either, and it was running unnecessary risks to be holding anyone by the arm.

"Nothing of the sort," said Bellag emphatically, stamping her foot. "He's as wise as either of you."

Before either of them could retort Habakkuk himself came in, stealthily, "I got it," he whispered, and from beneath his coat he produced the melodeon which did such valiant service the night of the barbecue.

"Can we not get married without frivolity?" said the Missionary sternly.

"There's been dancing at weddings since ever I can remember," retorted his sister. Habakkuk by way of reply squeezed the first few notes of a reel from his ancient box — it was simpler than talking anyway — and Katag an incipient hooch on her lips, spun round in the middle of the floor.

The Missionary averted his eyes. He was in no position to do anything more drastic. If Bellag was deserting him to marry Habakkuk, Katag had him at her mercy until they were formally married, but then, the Missionary promised himself, the work of reclamation would begin.

"Will I p-p-p-play you a p-p-proper t-t-tune?" asked Habakkuk, his silver horse-shoe moustaches dancing a reel of their own as he struggled to speak.

"Do," said Bellag, while Katag went on in some tuneless ballet of her own, round and round her outraged bridegroom. Before Habakkuk could make up his mind what tune to play, his sister Peigi came hurrying in, dragging Cold Murdo after her, so that it almost looked as if his legs were trailing along the ground, like a cod or ling, carried in the approved fashion by the gills, the tail writing its signature in the dust. If the truth were told, however, Murdo was not being dragged: he was clinging to Peigi for dear life, for he found himself in the same exposed situation as the Missionary.

"He asked me to marry him," announced Peigi as she came through the door.

"Maggie bolted," said Cold Murdo half apologetically, by way of explanation.

"Do you think it's Finch?" asked the Missionary in a conspiratorial whisper. Maggie Moogish, the outspoken, was the one person in the village who had ever given a hint of matrimonial aspirations. It had been a grave scandal in the village that she had once been seen to smile to Finch when they spoke together at a fanking.

"That reminds me," said Habakkuk, and he handed back the Missionary's murtair.

In his anxiety to conceal the tell-tale weapon from Cold Murdo who might, by the look of things, be a game-keeper's wife's uncle at any moment now, the Missionary dropped the murtair on the floor, and Katag grabbed it.

"That's no implement for a Missionary to use," she said. The Missionary knew it was no implement to parade in public, but he saw no harm in having it or using it. He sensed that there was going to be difficulty between himself and Katag. She had been brought up, in the tradition of the Post Office, to a rigid observance of the civil law, but a certain laxity in regard to the moral law. She frowned on poaching but it appeared she tolerated dancing at a reiteach. The Missionary, on the other hand, was brought up in the tradition of the church, which regarded the moral law as inflexible and imperative, whereas the civil law was man made and fallible — there was no commandment against poaching.

While the Missionary wrestled silently with these profundities, and Habakkuk struggled for courage to strike up a really lively tune on the melodeon, for which his love had been so long suppressed, and the two women gabbled in a corner about the details of their trousseau, Maggie Moogish was returning, anxious and humiliated, from her interview with Finch.

She had found the game-keeper in an even more surly mood than usual. Rather than face the jeers of the villagers, after the fiasco of the prosecution, he had sent in his resignation, and was busy packing his household effects in a few old tea chests. Maggie, with all her outspokenness, never got within a hundred miles of proposing to him. She simpered and he growled until she saw it was hopeless, and disappeared sorrowfully into the storm.

She was conscious, as she walked, of an unusual stir in the village, a constant to-ing and fro-ing of agitated people, like ants at a busy crossing near their hill.

Meesh was even more sorrowful than Maggie, and a good deal wetter as he struggled across the open moor. Unlike Maggie he was not yet aware there was anything unusual afoot in the village. But he soon found out.

Chapter XXV

The house was in darkness when Meesh reached it, and the fire was almost out. He was glad in a way that Annie wasn't on guard to receive him, but he could have done with a nice cheery blaze to dry off his sodden clothes before going to bed.

He was still sprawling helplessly in the dark looking for a box of matches, when the door opened and Willie came anxiously in, shining a powerful torch.

"You're back," he said, with relief in his voice. The sulks in which they parted were gone.

"What's left of me," said Meesh, with the ghost of a smile.

Willie was sorry for the old salt, but he could hardly keep from laughing as he looked at the intricate pattern traced out on the kitchen floor by the stream of water from Meesh's coat-tail as he hunted for the matches.

"Man," he said, in a fair imitation of Meesh's voice, "it's for all the world like a map of the children of Israel wandering in the wilderness for forty years."

As soon as he said it, Willie felt he had been rather heartless. Meesh was genuinely distressed by fatigue, and his face was all splattered with mud: he had fallen in the bog, perhaps more than once.

"I was worried about you," said Willie sincerely. "I've been watching for your light all night."

"I've been fifteen times round the Horn," said Meesh, trying to summon up a little of his usual gaiety. "I sailed in windjammers. I was in a typhoon in the China seas, and a hurricane in Jamaica, but this is the worst night I ever spent in my life."

"My poor feet," he added feelingly as he emptied a quart of brown peaty water from each of his sea-boots.

"I've had my fun, Willie, but it wasn't worth it."

"I warned you," said Willie.

"I know, I know," said Meesh, "You're a budding lawyer, and I'm just an old fool." It was said with all solemnity, but Willie wondered whether there wasn't a barb in it somewhere for all that.

"One thing I'm glad for," he added, "Annie's in bed. I thought she would be sitting up for us, scared we had fallen in the river."

"You don't know about Annie?" asked Willie, approaching the subject cautiously, as if he were breaking the news of an unexpected bereavement.

"What about her?" asked Meesh, still busy with his wet clothes, and paying little attention.

"She's not home yet. There hasn't been a light on here tonight," said

Willie taking another cautious step towards the calamitous news.

"I wouldn't worry about that," said Meesh quite gaily. "Someone must be sick in the village. It's just like Annie to stay when there's trouble."

"She generally leaves a note on the mantlepiece," he added, indicating Willie to have a look.

"There's a note here all right," said Willie, taking Annie's letter from the mantlepiece.

"An envelope?" said Meesh. "She's getting extravagant in her old age. Generally she just leaves a scribble on a piece of paper bag, or the edge of a newspaper, 'Bellag broke her leg' or 'Maggie has the mumps' or something like that."

Meesh was really puzzled by Annie's extravagance: it was so out of character. Then he exploded in a vast guffaw. "Willie, I've got it — it's her reply to the advertisement."

Willie knew better, but he said nothing.

"Man," said Meesh, sloughing off his tiredness, "I'll have to go to Crogorm again — I missed the post office — but it's worth it. Annie's proposal!"

He rubbed his hands with glee. "Willie," he said. "Do you think I'm mentioned. 'I have a brother, he's as much good to me as an old boot'!"

Willie still held his peace.

"I can hardly wait until it comes back from the paper," said Meesh, wringing one of his sodden stockings until it ran like Niagara into the basin.

Then Willie broke the news. "You don't need to wait," he said. "The letter is addressed to you."

"Me?" asked Meesh, thoroughly startled. In a flash he saw his whole world in chaos about him. He tore the envelope open, read quickly through the letter, then handed it to Willie, without a word.

It read, "My Dear Brother, I am very happy to know that you are looking about you for a wife, who will be a comfort to you in your old age, but there was no need to hide it from your own sister. Nothing would please me better than to see you comfortably settled. Don't worry about me. I've always had a fancy for the Postmaster. I know he has flighty notions about the District Nurse, but I'm going down to see him tonight to arrange for an early wedding, Your loving sister, Annie."

"I like the way she arranges other people's weddings. She's worse than yourself, Meesh," said Willie.

"Willie, what will I do?" asked Meesh, flummoxed for the first time in his life.

"Marry!" said Willie, in just the tone Meesh had used to the Postmaster earlier in the evening. It was cruel, but he could not resist the temptation.

"I'm too old for that," said Meesh. "I'll hate like the devil ending my days in the Poorhouse."

"Marry!" said Willie, still enjoying himself. "Marry as quick as you can!"

"No woman in her sense would take me," said Meesh with sincerity and candour. "I'm no more attractive than a bit of rotten cod."

Before Willie could think of a suitable comment, Meesh's words were disproved by the precipitate arrival of Maggie Moogish, out of breath, as if she had just completed an Olympic marathon.

"I came as soon as I saw your light," she gasped as she came through the door, and before Meesh could ask her why she came at all at three o'clock in the morning, she demanded, "What on earth have you done to this village?"

"Done?" asked Meesh.

"There never was the madness like it. It went through the whole place like whooping cough. You would think they were catching it from one another."

"Catching what?" asked Meesh, completely out of his depth for once.

"I'm the only one that escaped," replied Maggie irrelevantly.

"Escaped?" asked Meesh, looking to Willie for enlightenment.

"Don't tell me you didn't hear that your sister is marrying the Postmaster?" asked Maggie.

"I know, I know," said Meesh impatiently.

"You wouldn't be palming Annie off on the Postmaster if you weren't on the look-out yourself," said Maggie. "That's what my uncle Murdo said. As soon as he heard that yourself and Annie and the Postmaster were all getting married, he went off and proposed to Peigi."

"Did she take him?" asked Meesh, as the truth began to dawn.

"She hadn't right said 'yes' when Habakkuk took his cap from the peg and out the door like lightning, up the brae to propose to Bellag."

Maggie had the order of events a little confused, but she was right on the fundamentals.

"Since six o'clock this evening it's been nothing but marrying and giving in marriage, as they say in the Bible. Every time a woman said 'yes' there was a brother, or an uncle, or a cousin, without a woman to look after him, so off he went like a frightened hare to see what he could do for himself."

The night is still known in the Highlands as "reiteach mor Crobuie", which might be rendered, "the mass betrothal in Crobuie". After several decades of stagnation and sterility, practically the whole village got engaged in one magnificent spree. Even Winter offered and was accepted. He was afraid it might be bigamy, because he had a vague recollection about a wedding in the Crimea, but as he thought it might possibly have been his grandfather's he decided to take the risk.

From house to house the little parties moved all night long, proposing and being accepted, congratulating and being congratulated, kissing and being kissed. The bung was out and life flowed through Crobuie in a vast froth of match-making and merriment.

Meesh's spirits rose at the recital. His eyes flashed from under the bushy eyebrows. His tired feet, his sodden clothes, were forgotten and at each new incident related by Maggie his great guffaw rang out louder than ever.

"Willie," he said, slapping his friend on the back with such violence that he almost knocked him over, "when I said I would start an earthquake, I sure meant an earthquake."

He was in such lively spirits that Willie began to wonder whether the old rogue might not have foreseen it all; and even planned it, but Maggie brought Meesh to earth with a tumble.

"Who's going to make your porridge in the morning, and milk the cow, and cut the peats, and plant the potatoes?" she asked.

Meesh was silent. For the moment he had forgotten that he was losing Annie.

"You needn't think you'll squat down on the Postmaster," she added. "He made that quite clear to Annie."

"I'm going to bed," replied Meesh. His tiredness had suddenly returned and he looked quite dispirited again.

"I'll make you a cup of tea before you go," said Maggie with a purposeful voice. Before Meesh could restrain her, she darted into the scullery, and began to rummage among the crockery. "Where does Annie keep the teapot?" she shouted.

"I don't give a hang for teapots," replied Meesh angrily.

"I've got it," said Maggie, and Willie was quite surprised at the friendly warmth of her normally repellent voice. He had a sudden vision in his mind of the rose bushes in their garden at home, dry, thorny sticks, in the early spring, then suddenly one day there was a little fresh, pink tip at the growing points, and one knew that in a few months there would not only be leaves, but blossom. As Crobuie wakened from its trance, the people were changing, not only in their minds, but in their bodies. Nature, thwarted for so long, was reasserting itself.

"Where do we keep the sugar in this house?" sang out Maggie cheerily, and Willie could feel the change in her tone from speech to speech, almost from word to word.

Meesh said nothing. He was aware of the change just as surely as Willie, but the little word "we" still sounded like doom.

"I could understand you making the mistake, you're only an educated man, but after all I'm a sailor," he said irrelevantly to Willie.

"What mistake?" asked Willie.

"I forgot boomerangs," said Meesh in a bronach* voice, but with just that hint of acquiescence which made Willie feel that he welcomed the fate that was closing in on him.

"Here's the hot water bottle," shouted Maggie triumphantly. "I'll fill it for you when the kettle boils."

"There are worse things in life than a wooden leg," said Meesh abruptly. "Such as?" asked Willie.

---

* sorrowful

"No leg at all," said Meesh, and Willie took the point: Maggie might have her faults, but she was a good housekeeper, and beggars can't be choosers.

"It's Finch himself that would be jealous if he could see his girl friend now, filling a hot water bottle for an eligible bachelor like myself," said Meesh with a wink at Willie.

"That trash!" said Maggie with a flicker of the old ill-temper. "I'll boil a kettle for him right enough, but not to fill a bottle."

Meesh and Willie both knew in a flash that Maggie had tackled Finch and been rebuffed. It might have hurt the pride of an ordinary man to realise that he was only the consolation prize, but Meesh was intensely practical. He was never bothered by regrets or might have beens. His one purpose in life was to squeeze as much juice as possible from the orange in his hand.

"Listen," said Willie, suddenly, "that's a melodeon."

"So it is," said Maggie, not pausing in her chores, as if a melodeon at three o'clock in the morning were a common occurrence in Crobuie.

"I can see torches," said Willie at the window, excitedly. There was quite a line of torches strung out along the road, bobbing up and down as they approached, for all the world like a convoy of ships, rising and falling with the ground swell. The rain had taken off, the wind had dropped, and two or three stars were showing overhead as if someone had thrust a fist through the clouds.

"They're coming to serenade us," said Meesh, now glowing with pleasure. His prank had snowballed into something far bigger than he ever visualised, but it was still his prank.

At the head of the procession walked Habakkuk with his melodeon, Bellag half a step behind, leaving her arm free for action, but still proclaiming to the world her proprietary interest. Behind them came Annie and the Postmaster, arm in arm, then the Missionary and Katag, Winter and Chrissie Macluggage, old Christina and the Blacksmith, the whole village in fact, two by two, not walking or hobbling as was their wont, but skipping like lambs in time with the music. Even the Missionary made a token concession to the general air of festivity, by taking an occasional awkward hop, while Winter astonished them by playing leap frog with his stick.

Meesh rubbed his hands with glee. "I can't remember anything like this since the year I was wrecked in the Pacific, and the girls in grass skirts . . ."

His reminiscence was rudely interrupted by Maggie. "Never mind the girls in grass skirts," she said, firmly, but not unkindly. "Just let me smooth your hair before the guests come in to the reiteach."

Meesh submitted with a look of complete contentment. The Crobuie folk are fatalists: they take what the good Lord sends them — even Maggie Moogish for a wife.

The melodeon stopped abruptly, as Habakkuk stepped aside to let Annie and the Postmaster enter first.

"I told you, dearest, you didn't need to worry about him," said the Postmaster indicating Meesh, standing with Maggie by his side to receive the guests, as if they were an old married couple.

"It's myself that's glad to see them hitting it off so well," said Annie.

"Where will I find his underclothes when I need a change?" asked the practical Maggie.

"Take in a reef or two my girl," said Meesh unable to resist the opportunity for making a little scene. "We're not married yet!"

"We soon will be," said Maggie, unmoved. "I might as well know where to find things. It'll save time after the wedding."

"How would you like it," she added, "if I had to go over to the Post Office, on a Sunday morning, to ask for a clean shirt, and you shivering on the floor in your drawers and the church bells ringing?"

A great guffaw of laughter swept through the room, in which Meesh joined as heartily as anyone. There were no church bells in Crobuie, and never had been, but everyone seemed to take it for granted that there would be church bells in future and all sorts of marvels, now that the long night of desolation was over.

Chapter XXVI

There was one minor hitch which threatened the peace of the evening, but skilful generalship by Annie averted a catastrophe. In a way it was she who started the trouble, but she quickly realised what she had done, and retrieved the error.

The fun was growing fast and furious. On the night of the barbecue there had been an orderly progress of events, and an air of solemnity hung over the feast even during the singing and dancing, but on the night of the reiteach, good spirits brimmed over. Everyone was talking at once, singing at once, dancing at once, but no one listened to what anyone else was saying, they all sang different songs, and the dances were improvised as they went, although one might have suspected that they bubbled up from the deep, primeval recesses of a pagan folk-memory.

Meesh looked round the room and rubbed his hands. He never could resist a merry crowd. "It's going to be hard on the chickens," he said. "But boy, oh boy, what a hangover!"

It was then that Annie touched off the explosion with a seemingly innocent remark. "We're having champagne for the toasts," she said, with a hint of smugness. She felt that something a little more distinguished than usual was required at the Postmaster's wedding.

"I'll have a long white train," said Maggie, taking up the bidding at once. In a second the room was like some nightmare version of the fat stock sales, with a ring full of auctioneers, all calling their bids at once, but no buyers, and no cattle, unless the men looking glumly on might be counted in one of these categories.

"I'm having three bridesmaids," said Bellag desperately, and no one saw the absurdity of speaking about bridesmaids in a village where all the women were brides.

"I'm having four," said Chrissie Macluggage, unimaginatively, but in the famous foghorn voice that momentarily drowned every other sound in the room.

"I'm having a flower girl," retorted Bellag.

"I'm having a page," yelled Chrissie.

"We're sending out printed invitations with gold embroidery on them," said Katag, not sure of the technical terms, but determined that the wedding of the Missionary with the Postmaster's sister must be the grandest of them all — there were two separate claims to distinction.

"I'm having a cake with candles," Peigi chiming in.

"Isht, you fool," said Maggie, unkindly. "A cake with candles is only for a birthday."

"I don't care whether it's for a birthday or a funeral," retorted Peigi. "And what's more, Cold Murdo will put on the kilt, and that's more than anyone else can do — he's the only one in the village that was ever in the Seaforths."

Maggie laughed mockingly. "If you think my uncle is going to wear his kilt, you're far mistaken. I cut it up years ago to make a tartan tea cosy for my cousin in Philadelphia, and I made a petticoat for myself out of the bit that was left."

She skittishly raised her skirt to prove her point, and complete Peigi's discomfiture.

"Man," said Meesh to Willie, "did you ever see the hens fighting when you throw them a handful of meal."

Willie laughed, but the battle around them grew fiercer.

Then Annie intervened. "We'll have to send telegrams to each other," she said. The reading of telegrams had always been a feature of the Crobuie weddings, but it was a little preposterous to suggest that, when the whole village was getting married on the same day, each couple should send a telegram to all the others wishing them well. Annie knew the logic was a little bit askew, but she had her own purpose.

"And presents too," said Bellag at once.

The bidding might continue, but now the rivalry was gone! Annie smiled inwardly.

"We'll have to ask everyone in the parish from Crogorm to Crodubh," said Maggie expansively, and so it went on, absurdity heaped on absurdity as they planned the most lavish wedding the Highlands had ever seen.

But if Annie averted one crisis she precipitated another.

"It's going to be a very expensive business," said Cold Murdo in a lull. That was how all the men were feeling. In fact they could see that there was quite a lot to be said for calling the whole thing off, and going back to the women they had.

"Expensive," retorted Maggie, almost spitting with venom and contempt. The women sprang on Murdo like a pack of wolves.

"Talking about money and you getting married," yelled Chrissie Macluggage in a voice that stopped the clock and set the ornaments dancing on the mantleshelf.

"The tinkers themselves have more sense of decency," said Maggie returning to the attack.

"Grudging a few shillings for your own wedding," said Bellag with a sneer.

Cold Murdo had felt the violence of his niece's tongue on many occasions in the past, but seldom had he seen her in such a fury. The women were not going to be cheated of their men, or their marriage, at this late hour.

"Shillings," said Murdo, standing his ground. "You can't have all that nonsense and cakes and whisky for less than a hundred pounds."

"It would put a new gable in the church what you're thinking of spending

on idle frivolity;' said the Missionary in the same voice as he used for .
wake. "You might as well pour your money into the sea."

The argument grew fast and furious. The singing and dancing stopped
entirely. The party split up into agitated groups each arguing heatedly sex
against sex. Tables were thumped and fingers were pointed. Men swore and
women shrieked.

"Another fifty seconds and they'll use their claws;' said Meesh to Willie
in a delighted whisper, as he hurried from group to group throwing petrol
on the flames.

"It'll do them good to get all the venom out of the system before they
settle down in harness;' he explained to Willie, now thoroughly alarmed.
Unless something happened quickly there would be no harness, thought
Willie.

"Stop quarrelling now, and we'll drink a toast to each other;' said Annie,
the resourceful.

Arguing had made them all dry, and a hush fell on the gathering.

"Some toast;' said Meesh. "There's nothing in this house but cold tea."

"I have wine and I have whisky;' said Annie, curtseying to him gaily.
Meesh gaped in astonishment.

"I got them the day you sent the advertisement off — just in case;'
explained Annie.

Willie laughed, an unrestrained, hysterical laugh, as he thought of
Meesh's secrecy about the advertisement.

"My tongue has been hanging out for the last three months and you
wouldn't let me go to town for a dram;' said Meesh reproachfully.

"You took a dram too many the day you did go to town;' Annie reminded
him. Then relenting she added, "You can have one tonight."

"Just one, mind;' interposed Maggie, decisively.

"That's right;' said Annie, handing her responsibilities to the bride-to-
be. "You keep him on a short tether."

Meesh for once was too slow with his retort. Before an idea formed,
Annie and the Postmaster had vanished into the kitchen, but at least he
was cheered by the sound of popping corks.

It was then the District Nurse arrived, spruce and cheerful, as if she were
on a tour of duty in the middle of the afternoon, instead of on the wrong
side of breakfast time. She wanted to see the Postmaster as chairman of
the nursing committee, and, so many odd things had happened in the course
of the night, no one thought it funny that she should choose that time
and place for her interview. But still they were curious to know her business.

"Is it urgent?" asked Katag, cautiously.

"It's my resignation;' said Marion as she stepped into the kitchen.

"I wonder why is she resigning?" asked Katag, puzzled.

"Tamailt*;' said Maggie. "She's the only old maid in the village now."
Having so nearly missed that fate herself, Maggie had a better appreciation
than most of the terror it held.

* chagrin

"I don't think it's that at all," said Meesh, once more in control of events.

"Neither do I," said Cold Murdo, sagely.

"What is it, darling?" asked Peigi, and Murdo blushed.

"Figure it out for yourself," said he. "Twenty three weddings in one month! Would you like to be District Nurse?"

"It's not that either," said Meesh when the laughter had died away.

"What is it then?" asked Murdo a little testily.

"Ask Willie," said Meesh, thrusting the embarrassed lad into the centre of the room. As Marion returned from the kitchen, helping Annie and the Postmaster with the glasses, Meesh gave Willie another push.

"Go on, kiss her," he said.

Instead Marion threw her arms round Meesh's neck, and kissed him warmly on the cheek.

"Meesh, you're a darling," she whispered.

For the first and last time in his life, Meesh blushed.

Chapter XXVII

Midway between the reiteach and the wedding came the night which is still remembered in Crobuie as "the fire of the sticks." Meesh planned it, with more than usual care, for he attached great importance to it, but of course, none of the others realised that it had been planned, or what the purpose was when they took part. Even Willie was fooled to begin with.

On the morning after the reiteach, he met Meesh hobbling through the village on a stick, more bent, more rheumaticky, more bronach, than Winter himself.

Willie smiled. He had never seen Meesh use a stick before. Indeed Meesh was notorious in the village for not using one — a departure from the accepted mores which was regarded as eccentric, and possibly even heretical. It was certainly non-conformity of a very public, and therefore, very dangerous type. On one occasion the Missionary had read through the book of Deuteronomy to see whether the use of a walking stick was obligatory, but he had to confess that he found no text which went quite so far, although there were one or two which were very near it, if one viewed them in the proper light. Not everyone could see in the words what the Missionary saw. He was more skilful with texts than the Blacksmith was with iron. The summit of the Blacksmith's achievement was to take a plain bar, and shape it into a horseshoe, but the Missionary could work an even more remarkable transformation on a plain piece of Scripture, without aid of fire or bellows.

Willie was surprised when he saw Meesh hirpling on his stick. "That'll teach you to go traipsing to Crogorm," he said, a little unkindly. He assumed that Meesh was too tired to walk without artificial aid, after his journey through the storm and the bog.

Meesh smiled. "Did you ever see the sleeping beauty?" he asked irrelevantly.

"No," said Willie.

"I thought not," said Meesh. "But no doubt you've read the story."

"I suppose I have," said Willie. "Or else I had it read to me."

"That's the worst of being an educated man," said Meesh gravely. "You've read everything, but you know nothing. Now, if you were a travelled man like me, you might even have seen the Sleeping Beauty."

"Where did you see her?" asked Willie with a laugh.

"I can't remember where," said Meesh, as if making a valiant effort to recollect. "It was a long, long, time ago."

"It must have been before I cut my wisdom teeth," he added, darting a sharp glance at Willie from beneath his bushy eyebrows. "Anyway, the point is that they've got it wrong in the story book."

"In what way," asked Willie humouring the old man.

"Well," said Meesh. "In the story book it's all very romantic when the Prince kisses her, and she wakens up. Stuff and nonsense. She didn't even see the Prince when she wakened up. She was screaming her head off with the cramp. You just try it. Sleep for a hundred hours, let alone a hundred years, and you'll know what cramp is."

"Is that what's wrong with you?" asked Willie pointing to the stick.

"No," said Meesh emphatically, "but that's what's wrong with Crobuie. You remember the way they were after the barbecue? They'll be ten times worse this morning."

Willie understood. Coming to life was not an easy process for Crobuie. The sleep had been too long and too deep. It was a shock to find that what they thought was the long twilight of approaching death was really a belated dawn, with another day to face.

"I never pictured you in the role of Prince Charming," said Willie, standing back to survey the weather-beaten old seaman, who looked as little like a fairy book prince as anyone could.

"Kissing is not my line," said Meesh, with a deprecating wave of his hand. "But there's such a thing as alarm clocks."

"Alarm clocks?" asked Willie, puzzled.

"You know the things," said Meesh impatiently, as if instructing a child. "They go tick, tick, tick, and then they make a noise like all the devils in hell, and before you know it, you're awake."

"I still don't see the point," said Willie.

"There's more than one way of wakening a sleeping beauty," said Meesh. "I'm not much good at kissing, but I'm a dab hand at the winding."

Willie agreed. "You are that," he said heartily.

"Well, there you are," said Meesh, as if that explained everything. "I've set the alarm clock off, and now they're awake, but the cramp is something awful."

He held up his stick. "I want them to get used to seeing me with this, so that they'll all follow my lead the night I burn it."

"If you want to lead sheep my boy, you've got to be a sheep," he added sagely. "Or at least you've got to make them think you are."

One night, about ten days later, the whole male population of Crobuie gathered on the machair near the spot where they held their barbecue, and solemnly burnt their walking sticks. Meesh discussed it with no one: suggested it to no one. He simply went down to the machair when he thought the time was ripe, and began to chop his walking stick into firewood.

In a few moments the men began to gather round like curious cows, and when they saw what was afoot they all got busy with hatchets themselves. The bonfire was well ablaze before they had time to wonder how they would ever walk home without their sticks, and then, to their great astonishment, they realised that they were walking without them already, with the greatest of ease. With returning life the sticks had become an encumbrance, although they did not know it. Even Winter straightened up like a willow branch that is held and then released, and from that moment he ceased to talk of the Crimea. He knew in a flash that it was not he, but his grandfather, who had been there, and anyway it wasn't the Crimea, but South Africa in the Boer war.

Once the sticks were alight the men heaped all the combustible rubbish they could find on the bonfire: armfuls of heather, ancient wheelbarrows, the thatch from disused barns. As the bonfire grew, the frenzy grew, and they gave themselves up to an orgy of burning.

There was a great crackling and sparks rose high on the evening air. Acrid smoke drifted across the village drawing the women to the doors. In a few moments they joined the men but they did not come empty-handed. As if by one accord, they cast all their drab, black clothes on the bonfire. In the leaping light of the flames, Willie saw them arrayed for the first time in brightly coloured garments. They looked young again, and beautiful. It was then, for the first time, he realised how deep was the psychological disorder in a people who perfected the tartans and the eightsome reel, and then took to black clothes and long faces, as if life were a disaster.

The bonfire fulfilled some primitive need in the soul. It was a ritual of renewal, helping them to slough off the old encrusted habits of a dying community, and re-adapt themselves to life. Although none of them put it in words, none of them even knew it in their conscious minds, they were ceremonially burning the dead wood from their long frustrated lives. A new Crobuie was rising Phoenix-like from the ashes.

"You can't teach an old dog new tricks," said Meesh to Willie in a whisper. "Unless you know how!" he added slyly.

Willie marvelled at the insight of the old rascal. The village had been drifting towards the abyss for years. To row against the tide was a great physical effort, but a greater mental effort was required to make the attempt. The Gaelic proverb says of any difficult task "it's a day's work to begin." Willie, better than most, realised that it took a heroic effort for Crobuie to face up to life again.

The excitement rose with the flames. Habakkuk's melodeon, and the mysterious bagpipes from the barbecue, set everyone dancing. The music was inspired, but even more remarkable was the fact that Habakkuk lost his stammer just as Winter lost his stoop. Sometimes in later years he pretended that it had come back, just to set his silver horse-shoe moustaches going, and give the village fun, but from the night of the bonfire he had full command of his tongue.

There was no hangover after the bonfire as there had been after the barbecue. Crobuie awakened in the morning with anxious thought about the reckless actions of the night, but it was soon discovered that nothing had been burnt which anyone really missed and the village looked fresher and tidier than it had for fifty years.

The past died for good in the flames, and Crobuie, without inhibition or misgiving, prepared for the greatest wedding feast in the history of the Highlands. People no longer felt that it was a guilty thing to be alive. Oddly enough, when restraint was withdrawn, the temptation to excesses disappeared as well.

The bonfire — symbolic, like the pillar of fire in the Bible — was seen at Crogorm and Crodubh. It looked as if the whole of Crobuie had gone up in flames, and the anxious villagers set off across miles of moorland in the dark, to rescue whom they could. When they arrived, and saw what was going on, they joined in the jollification.

It was then, for the first time, they heard the story of the reiteach mor, and were greatly astonished, for Crobuie was notorious even in the west for its backwardness and lack of enterprise.

The news spread like a prairie fire. Long before dawn on the day of the wedding, crowds were converging on Crobuie from every point of the compass. From neighbouring islands came a long procession of boats, down to the gunwale with men, women, children and collie dogs, coming to marvel and join in the fun.

The village was decorated with flags. Hundreds of guns — none of them licensed — were fired as the procession of newly married couples emerged from the little village church. There was feasting, dancing and song, all through the night and far into the following day. There was no barn or building in Crobuie large enough to hold the guests, but the night was fine, and they danced on the machair by the light of the moon.

They might be dancing yet, for that matter. Life in Crobuie has never been the same again. If ever you feel weary and beset in spirit, seek it out, and have a word with Meesh.

It is not an easy place to find. It is still without telephone or road. It appears on no map. Ask in the villages round about and they will tell you blankly, "I never heard of it," but it is there, somewhere in the west, in that enchanted land between the Butt of Lewis and Barra Head. Nothing would please me better than to take your hand and lead you to it, but unfortunately, I've forgotten the way myself.

But look for it by all means, and one day, if you're lucky, you may find Meesh leaning by the peat stack, smoking his pipe.

Or his ghost!

Meesh and his world have long since vanished but his spirit of fun lives on.